TH[ ] OF
DOCTOR BILL SHAKES
AND THE
MAGNIFICENT IONIC PENTATETRAMETER

A STEAMPUNK SHAKESPEARE ANTHOLOGY

EDITED BY MATTHEW DELMAN & JAYMEE GOH

The Omnibus of Doctor Bill Shakes
and the Magnificent Ionic Pentaterameter
ISBN (print): 978-0-9853857-0-5
ISBN (ePub): 978-0-9853857-1-2

Published by Doctor Fantastique Books

Copyright ©2012 by The Doctor Fantastique Company

Produced in Massachusetts

All works ©2012 by their authors.

All works in this book are steampunk derivatives of the public domain works of William Shakespeare. All events portrayed in this book are fictitious. Any reference to historical events, real people, or actual locales are used fictitiously. Other names, places, characters, and incidents are the products of their respective writers' imaginations, and any resemblance to actual locales, events or persons, living or dead, are coincidental. Maybe.

Every reasonable attempt has been made to identify owners of copyright. Errors or omissions will be corrected in subsequent editions.

Introduction ©2012 by Mike Perschon

Cover art ©2012 by Monica Marier

Doctor Fantastique Books ©2011
The Doctor Fantastique Company

28/11/2012 70

"There was never yet philosopher
That could endure the toothache patiently."
      MUCH ADO ABOUT NOTHING
              V, i, 35

Contents

INTRODUCTION
BY MIKE PERSCHON 1

THE TRAGIC TALE OF KING LEAR'S WONDERS
BY JENNIFER CASTELLO 7

"DEVOURING TIME, RUST THOU THE ROBOT'S GEARS"
BY OLIVIA WAITE 25

MEASURE FOR STEEL-SPRUNG MEASURE
BY REBECCA FRAIMOW 27

"WHERE ART THOU MUSE THAT FORGET'ST ME SO LONG?"
BY TUCKER CUMMINGS 35

THE MALEFACTION OF TYBALT'S MECHANICAL ARMATURE
BY TIM KANE 37

"NOT FROM THE STARS DO I MY JUDGEMENT PLUCK"
BY J.H. ASHBEE 51

JULIUS C-ZR
BY BRET JONES 53

"Your expanse of metal is a waste of time"
by Frances Hern..73

Much Ado About Steam Presses: A Scandal of Minor Importance
by R. J. Booth..75

"My brasswork's gleam is nothing like the sun"
by Alia Gee 99

Leo's Mechanical Queen
by Claudia Alexander..101

"A woman's face with artist's sure hand painted"
by J.H. Ashbee 135

The Misfiring Love-Piston of Sir John Autumnrod
by Larry Kay..137

"Not iron, nor the Difference Engine"
by Kelly Fineman 173

What You Fuel
by Jaymee Goh 175

"To me, fair friend, you never can be old"
by Tucker Cummings... 189

A Midsummer's Night Steam
by Scott Farrell 191

"Devouring Time, wear thou steam-hammer's head"
by J.H. Ashbee 227

Richard, Dismantled
by Jess Hyslop 229

ABOUT THE AUTHORS AND SONNETEERS 245

ABOUT THE EDITORS 251

Introduction
by Mike Perschon

My wife and I celebrated our fifteenth anniversary by attending a performance of Shakespeare's *Twelfth Night* in one of our city parks. Could there be anything more romantic to an English lit prof than to attend one of the world's great comedic masterpieces while the sun sets on the Edmonton river valley? Arguably, there are other equally romantic outings, especially considering the plague of mosquitos that assailed the audience throughout the performance. But we were treated to a double delight: the costumer for this performance of *Twelfth Night* had chosen steampunk as her design aesthetic.

While it lacks any air of *amour*, I couldn't help but mentally compare this production's use of the steampunk aesthetic with another rendering of *Twelfth Night* I'd come across online, which made *Twelfth Night* look like *Hamlet* or *Macbeth*. The excessive use of black in the steampunk costumes was oppressive, dystopic, hardly Illyrian. The Shakespeare-in-the-Park costumes were a riot of colour, a pastiche of fabric and accessory: Feste evoked shades of *The Road Warrior*'s gangly gyro-captain, while Toby Belch and Andrew Aguecheek sported attire covered in a rainbow of oversaturated colours worthy of a Rio Carnivale float. I wondered whether the audience for the Stygian-garbed version found it as easy as I to differentiate between the characters. My Olivia went from mourning-black to coquettish-pink to tell her tale. The online Olivia went from black to black.

I share this anecdote to demonstrate that steampunk is an aesthetic that can be applied to great effect or utter vanity. In one case, the steampunk seems to add nothing to our understanding of the story or communication of theme. When Sebastian and Viola were shipwrecked at the start of the play, actors in a cardboard Harper-Goff *Nautilus* raced past us, screaming. The audience might not know *steampunk*, but they know Disney-does-Verne, and they understood the sub was about to founder. While they likely wondered about all those goggles, the ridiculous number of extra lenses and geegaws on Feste's produced laughter, which is arguably what an actor wants *every* time he walks onstage as Feste. The cast could have been the most sober lot of gloomy Gusses to ever see the stage, and the costumes would have screamed joviality and Bacchanal anyhow.

That is what the authors, poets, and editors of *The Omnibus of Doctor Bill Shakes* have ostensibly set out to do. Whether they succeed or not is up to the individual reader, and I would be remiss to suggest otherwise, given the range of approaches within these pages.

Jennifer Castello's "The Tragic Tale of King Lear's Wonders" starts our journey strong, doing more than simply slapping gears on the Bard's pen, but troubling both the Shakespearean and steampunk waters with a challenge for *making* of a more wondrous kind. Olivia Waite and Tucker Cummings' poetry provide whimsical and grave bookends to Rebecca Fraimow's "Measure for Steel-Sprung Measure," which imagines a secondary world where becoming a clockwork golem is either sublime choice or infernal punishment. All three form a trilogy of clockwork devices as paths to various immortalities. Tim Kane's "The Malefaction of Tybalt's Mechanical Armature" re-imagines the tragic duel between Romeo and Tybalt, while retaining much of the original Bard's Elizabethan verse in its dialogue. The stories and poems vacillate from humourous to grim, from devotion to Shakespeare's meter and rhyme to playful paraphrases that sometimes subvert the original story, allowing us to see it from a new perspective.

Above all, what this anthology does is show us once again the diversity of application for the steampunk aesthetic: at times, the steampunk aesthetic can be as slapped on as cogs-on-a-stick, while in others, it is woven into the tale or poem's thematic thrust. In either case, we are dealing with steampunk. In the case of *The Omnibus of Doctor Bill Shakes*, we get a little of both in varying degrees. This isn't to say that any of these are cog-on-a-stick, but some, such as Alia Gee's "My brasswork's gleam is nothing like the sun," are enjoyable for the same reason I like to hear a cover song, to see what minor changes have been wrought; or in the case of Bret Jones' "Julius C-ZR," the story and underlying themes remain the same, only now there are airships where a Roman galley might have been–Caesar/C-ZR still needs to die, and the reasons are largely the same. Others are epiphanies of a counterfictional sort, addressing the "what if?" of alternate history to Shakespearean history, not ours, such as Castello's aforementioned take on *King Lear*.

In doing this, *The Omnibus of Doctor Bill Shakes* exemplifies what Istvan Csicsery-Ronay Jr. says about steampunk, that the focus is "not on what might have been historically possible, which would suppose the discourse of historical realism. Instead, they focus on the imaginatively possible, a dialectical mesh of fantasies... as both the Victorians themselves and *fin de millennium* U.S. techno-bohemians might imagine them" (109). Steampunk has been mixing the literary with the historical since Jeter's *Morlock Night*, with its mash-up of Arthurian Legend, Vernian technology, and Wellsian time travel. Or as I stated in *Locus* magazine in September of 2011, "The mix of the historical and the literary have been the game of steampunk since its inception ... Steampunk offerings continue to utilize a mix of historical figures whose lives have become legend, and fictional heroes whose stories have become truth in the minds of their readers, carrying on the tradition of blurring the lines between fiction as history, and history as fiction." (40). Consider Larry Kay's dizzying mix of American Civil War personalities with *Henry IV* to see what I mean. This blending of alternative history and recursive fantasy is arguably at the core of the steampunk aesthetic: not what might have been in a world governed by natural sciences, but the Roburian heights one might achieve in Vernotopia, Perelandra, or Wold Newton.

Take this anthology as an example: it's not about

wondering what might have happened if Christopher Marlowe hadn't died at the age of 30, but rather imagining an Illyria filled with clockwork people speaking in iambic pentameter. And why shouldn't we? After all, the Bard didn't invent Illyria—he just borrowed it for his own ends, as have the offending shadows who offer up these visions, these weak and idle themes, for our delight.

Works Cited

Csicsery-Ronay Jr., Istvan. *The Seven Beauties of Science Fiction.* Wesleyan University Press, 2008.

Perschon, Mike. "Fictional Histories and Historical Fictions: Collisions in the Real and Imaginary in Steampunk." *Locus.* Sept 2011. 40.

The Tragic Tale of King Lear's Wonders
by Jennifer Castello

My mother once warned if I did not mind my manners, I would find my end in hell. And there in hell, I would only have madmen to serve.

I did mind my manners, and in doing so, I still ended here. But I suppose even the unlikeable sorts of fellows need those to follow them.

I am to be here. And so I stay.

If anyone finds this rather long scroll, I am aware they may not read the entirety. But I feel as if in England's discord, we need someone with sound mind to write down precisely what has recently unfolded instead of leaving it to the chance of papers or the Queens. Aye, neither could give you a good account. However, I assure you that I am trustworthy in my recounting.

My king now sits in this cave, out near the heath and far from any castle he's inhabited. You wouldn't recognize him as he is tonight; he's waterlogged, cragged in the face. His beautiful brass mechanisms he has clung to keeping, even when the weight of his own natural body became too much for us to lag. But now, they breathe air and fall green. His glorious metal arm, once ornate in the grandest of metals and gold and able to hold an entire nation above his crown, hasn't been able to move since we all tripped into the brook on our way up this hill. The Fool is attempting to unparalyze him, but your king is nothing more than an immobile old man with glassy eyes which can't tear themselves from the storm outside.

"My friend," he said to me only an hour ago. "How does the heath look upon this night?"

And although we'd just plodded through twenty stone-throws of said heath for the past evening to find shelter here, I ventured out to the mouth of the cave once more to have a look.

"It floods, your majesty," I said, pressing my palm on the cold rock of the entrance. And it did flood, the ground swallowing all those beautiful machines and factories we'd set on the grass and streams. The cranes above cranked and moaned with the weight of the wind, and the world began to tear apart at its welded seams.

"And the factories?" your king inquired.

"Rusting," I said.

Your king nodded quietly, and his glassy eyes looked to the fire I'd built for him. "I see," he said. And he shoveled his way into his corner. "Heaven's vault then cracks…" he muttered.

I would understand if you feel no pity in your heart for this man; he divided his nation into pieces as a boy would divide his cake. We have all suffered for his impetuousness, even my own self. But there is a slight difference between you and myself, friends: I was there as he split the cake.

Our kingdom has grown mighty under Lear's rule. No one can doubt that, regardless of their feelings about Lear. When England was a war-torn country after brutal beatings from neighbors and ungrateful bastards across the sea, Lear led us into a new century with one brilliant innovation after another. While Wordsworth disagreed with the push for the cities and factories, and found his solace in Tintern Abbey, the rest of us flourished. My own father found employment he wouldn't have found anywhere else in one of these machina assembly lines.

But there is no real cause to tell you the history you already know. I've gone to this narration to tell you of what you don't know.

I suppose I'll set us in the palace round December, when the winter's snow hurled through London with the force of a thousand steam engines. Spewing smoky white clouds from the west, the season charged through, littering our streets with mounds of icy patches and brown sludge. You could barely walk from the palace to the river without finding your feet frozen right to the bottom of your boots. But still, our king found it time for celebration.

"Give me the map there," Lear instructed me as we all congregated in his frigid study. I looked to the books and atlases surrounding us for stories high, and finally decided on the one Lear had haphazardly pointed to. In the candlelight, the old king unwound it and pressed his focals to his graying eyes. "We shall express our darker purpose," he muttered. "My friends, know that I have divided my kingdom in three, and this is my fast intent to shake all cares and business from my age. I shall confer said cares on younger strengths while we—now unburdened—crawl toward death."

Discomforted, the older gentlemen looked at one another, shifting their grins behind walrus moustaches to slight frowns. But Lear did not notice, he merely plowed on.

"We have this hour a constant will to know my daughters' several dowers, that future strife may be prevented now," Lear held his glorious, gilded machina of an arm above the map of his kingdom. Its brilliant golden embroidery glistened and danced in the candlelight, and all took pause to admire it. Many times it had been drawn, illustrated, even photographed. But nothing could outshine the true mighty right arm of the nation. It whirred and geared, nearly working just as well than the original he had lopped off and discarded for this new one's beauty.

As he took the quill in his metal fingers, the doors opened to three beautiful children. I dare say I slip by calling them children; they're nearly the age I was when I first came to work here in the palace.

Goneril, the most fearsome and eldest, adorned herself in brilliant hues of blue and silver. Atop her head shone golden pilot focals, goggled on a silken strap. This may not come to anything out of the ordinary to you, my friends; I'm sure we all know a lady who wears these goggles as a lovely accessory in the newest fashions. But my lady Goneril had earned hers, flying a zeppelin 'round the world and back again.

Regan, the most beautiful and middle child, robed herself in metallic armor and a welded eye which shone with the radiance of a red ruby. Her thin mouth curled into a deep crimson smile as she bowed low to her father with the grace only a Learian machina could support. Again, this eye may not surprise you or awe you in any way; many of our youngsters went about beautifying their faces years ago. But Regan's was the first.

And finally, little Cordelia entered the study. She was the youngest, and looked quite plain next to her elder sisters. Her blonde hair could have been made of a haystack, and her deep hazel eyes were nothing compared to the brilliance of a ruby. Her plain clothing did not exhibit anything but her task of rolling from bed and dressing herself. Her freckled cheeks were the only remarkable trait on her face, and nothing decorated her head but unruly curls.

"And here they are to answer," Lear gave a jolly laugh as he raised his arms in welcome. "My daughters, since now we will give you all rule, land, and cares of state... which of you shall we say doth love me most."

"Oh, it is myself, Father," Goneril's low, surly voice sung. "I have known our king the longest."

"But I hath spent the most days in the palace," Regan said.

"And who exhibits on her bosom the most brilliant and rarest exemplification of thy king's rule?" Lear inquired.

"Oh, it is myself, Father," Goneril argued once more. "I have the grandest of airships all with my father's name scrolled 'cross their bellies."

"But I hath the most factories here on earth," Regan said. "More than all my sister's ships combined."

Lear embraced his daughters, then turned to his heads of state. "Three kingdoms shall be made for three queens. But the largest bounty may extend where nature doth with merit challenge. Whichever holds the most love and reverence for my might shall hold the mightiest kingdom. Three days, three exhibitions. Goneril," he turned to the tallest. "Our eldest born shall speak first. Tomorrow, we shall begin."

—⚡—

My, it grows cold in this cave. Your king is near to sleep, and I find my own self growing weary. But his rest shall give me more time; as long as the Fool we've acquired continues to drink himself into a stupor, I shouldn't have any interruptions from my narrating.

—⚡—

The first day, we met at the sky docks. It was here we soared through the snowy clouds, our primped hair flooding down our face and into our eyes. It was always invigorating to blast up into the air, where only the adventuresome had the honor to live. I'd always found myself a bit sick after these trips to the airships, but there was something so grandiose and gorgeous about it all, I'd pay the price gladly.

For those of you who have never seen these beauties overhead, I shall describe to you the wonder of an airship. A large, helium-propelled balloon pressured from the inside, with two expansive wings reaching outwards and plucking up and down with the wind. Underneath stands the bulb, where women and men dress in silk and leather, their thin hands at the helm in almost (and sometimes quite literally) an extension of machina. It was with the airship fleet's cannon arsenal that France was thrown back to Gaul, and Germany back to Hungary. All round the world these days, look to the air and see the leather straps of the wings, the puttering steam engenius from the rudder... and Goneril stood atop it all, laughing with the shrill ecstasy of a child with the greatest toy ever crafted.

"The air!" Goneril pressed her whole body into the weight of the helm's turn, and we felt the ship sway to the port side and cut through a mountain made of clouds. "Sir, I do love you more than words can wield the matter!"

The airship groaned like a beast, breathing in the free winds as it cut past three of its brethren. The white horizon became a pasture for these magnificent animals as we all held onto the leather straps inside. She bucked her pet round, up and down, and finally in a brilliant loop.

Gloucester nearly lost his brunch.

Lear laughed, "It truly is a mighty thing–these creatures I tailored and you tame!"

Goneril's silk goggled focals wrapped round her blue eyes as her thin figure steadied herself and she planted her boots in place. One last turn, cutting through a storm cloud which had begun to form above the sea. Cornwall gave out a shriek as his wife dodged a sporadic electric bolt and threw the windows to a shower of rain. The great thunderclap sounded through our bones, nearly deafening us. But Goneril only gave a deep laugh and casually soared back to safety.

The airship now floated like a wispy bee as she

let go of her helm, removed her focals, and faced her father. Her ruddy cheeks and sparking eyes gave way to a large grin, and she spread her arms as she bowed to him.

"Dearer than eyesight," she began. "Dearer than eyesight, space, and liberty... beyond what can be valued, rich or rare, is the sky. This is my father's grandest achievement. Harnessing the kingdom we were to never see. So no less than life, with grace, health, beauty, honor... as much as child ever loved or father found..." She gestured to the expanse round her. "A love that makes breath poor and speech unbearable."

She stepped forward. "Beyond all manner of so much, I love you."

Lear's eyes melted into gracious tears, and he nodded. "Of all these bounds," he said, and I handed him his map. With his quill in his gilded hand, he drew the lines. "Even from this line to this... underneath the shadows of fleets, and rich with those who will follow you to stars... I make thee lady."

Little Cordelia now stood dumbfounded, and she looked to me with worried hazel eyes.

"What should I say to him? What should I show him?" Cordelia whispered, and I patted her haystack head.

"Regard how much you love him, and show this," I replied.

—⚋—

The second day was Regan's. We met in the heart of London, the clouds now no longer seen. Instead, there hovered a constant, thick frontline of soot and smoke coughing from the factory chimneys. Little boys covered in coal marched past us, and behind them came the walking metal behemoths which balanced on two legs and four guns. It were these machina which gave us India and Australia. A shot of hot steam came from their joints, and the clanking of their metal feet bore thick footprints in the muddy sludge and broken cobblestone. Even Gloucester's bastard son, donned in dapper bowler cap and monocle, looked quite terrified as we inched along their route to the beating core of the factories.

Regan, her ruby eye surveying the assembly lines, clanked her armor up the steel staircase as we followed behind. She threw her plated arm to bid us gaze at her father's empire. Hundreds–no, thousands of men and women marching and working as one. Cogs in wheels, simpering whistles, just like clockwork which never missed a minute.

"Sir!" Regan sounded mightily from her perch above the horde. "I am made of that same metal as my sister! So prize me at her worth! In my true heart, I find she names my very deed of love ... only she and her sky come too short."

Outside the plated window groaned another cold monster, roaring out pellets of fire from four unrusted wheels. Regan pressed her hands to her waist. "It was with the factories my father saved our kingdom! Not unlike thy army, I profess myself an enemy to all other joys which are not named King Lear!"

Lear roared a cry of satisfaction as he stood before his mighty military, and he embraced Regan in a deep affection.

"To thee and thine hereditary ever remain an ample third of our fair kingdom!" he ordered as I took his map to him once more. His quill made the lines near Goneril's. "No less in space, validity, and pleasure than that conferred on Goneril. You shall have the earth where we won our battles, all from London to Tintern Abbey."

Cordelia looked to me again. "My love's more ponderous than my tongue, Lord Kent." She shivered. "What shall I say tomorrow?!"

"As I said, little one," I assured her. "Use not your tongue, but the might of his creations. Your sisters have shown the might of his earth and his sky, now you must show him something more."

Cordelia nodded. "It's nearly impossible," she said. "My love's more richer than his might."

—⁂—

Aye, and it was. I wish I could have fashioned something more for Cordelia than what I did, and I regret leaving her to her own volition. For on the third day, we met at the palace where Cordelia led us to the study once more.

"Now, my joy," the old king beamed, opening his heart to his simple third daughter. "Although my last and least."

He took his quill one last time upon the map, and he poised it to cut the largest piece of the cake.

"What can you say to draw a third more opulent than your sisters? What can you show of my power and wonder to cut thyself a kingdom?"

Cordelia, her hair like hay and her dress not changed from the day before, lowered her head. Both her words and her display were silent and empty.

"Come, speak," Lear prodded. "What have you to say? What have you to show?"

Cordelia let out a rattling breath. "Nothing, my lord."

Lear stopped. He stared. "Nothing?"

"Nothing," she said.

"How?" Lear said. "Nothing will come of nothing. Speak again."

"Unhappy I am," she whispered as if she'd turned to a mouse. "I cannot heave my heart into my mouth nor into one of your great machina wonders. I love you, Your Majesty. Nothing can show how much, no wonderment of your saved kingdom can regale my heart… except for your grandest achievement."

Lear stared at her. "What is this."

"What you see before you," Cordelia said. "Flesh and blood made of love. Nothing more, nothing less."

"How," Lear said. "How, Cordelia! Mend your speech a little, lest you may mar your fortunes!"

"Good my lord, you have begot me, bred me, loved me," she said. "Nothing more, nothing less. Thine airships are powerful and graced us with the sky. Thine factories brought industry which graced us with as much land as the sun offers. But thy love–"

"Stop." Lear was red, and he could not look at his lords and dukes in this humiliation. "You have nothing to show us?"

"Nothing more or nothing less than what I have

here," she said.

"Goes thy heart with this?"

"Aye, my lord."

"So young and untender?"

"So young, my lord, and true. Unlike my sisters, I have no ruby eye, no silk goggled focals… but I have this. Nothing more, nothing less."

Lear's warm face grew cruel with his aged wrinkled frown. His graying eyes narrowed. His gilded fingers clenched a fist. And he turned from his daughter. "Let it be so," he scowled. "Thy truth then be thy dower. For by the sacred radiance of the sun, by all the operation of the Galvanic electrics from which we do exist and cease to be… Here I disclaim my paternal care–"

"Father!" Cordelia cried.

"And as a stranger to my heart and me, hold thee from this for ever!" he plowed forward.

"My liege!" I stepped forward as well, throwing Cordelia to my arms. "Think of what you say–"

"Peace, Kent!" Lear roared. "Come not between the dragon and his wrath! I loved her most!" He threw a reading stand to the ground in a clatter of shattered trinkets. "Hence avoid my sight!" he bellowed. "So be my grave my peace as here I give her father's heart from her!"

"Royal Lear!" I begged him. "Whom I have ever honored as my king, loved as my father, as my great patron–"

"The bow is bent and drawn! I will snap!"

"I will be quite unmannerly when Lear is mad!" I held the shaking, sobbing Cordelia. "What wouldst thou do, old man? Think'st thou that duty shall have dread to speak when power to flattery bows?"

"Kent, on thy life, no m—"

"Answer my life my judgment!" I spoke over his own voice. "Thy youngest daughter does not love thee least!"

"By God, I will strike you down!" And my king fell upon me with his metal arm. With a slam to my face, I fell to my knees. Cordelia shrieked. No other lord nor princess moved.

I gave a small sputter, blood rushing from my broken heart, and I looked to him. "By God, my friend?" I said. "You swear on God? Well, I swear as long as I am able to speak, I shall tell thee you are wrong."

Lear threw me once more to the wall with his metal arm, and Cordelia rushed to help me up. But the lot of them towered over us, striking us in their shadow as Lear raised his hand once more and pointed that gilded finger at my neck.

"Thou art banished," he hissed. "Five days I allot thee. Then thou art banished."

"Freedom lives hence," I said quietly. "And banishment is here."

—⚍—

The heath is ruthless this night. Lear weeps in his sleep. He mutters to himself feverishly. When I returned to our kingdom dressed as a peasant and found him at his Regan's palace, he was as much a stranger as I was to him in my disguise.

I tell you he cannot move that arm any longer. His eyes are all but faded over. His warm cheeks grow sick and white. His portly tub wanes to bones. And as you may find this a sweet vengeance for the civil war his daughters are poised to battle with his quilled lines, I find it breaking my heart.

"It was not supposed to end in this," Lear whispers to me now, fluttering in and out of sleep. "Goneril and Regan were to reign in peace—"

The airships sound their sirens above, shrouded by the electric storms and thunderclaps. Each hour at least, the lightning slashes one of her beasts and it falls to the heath, cowering into a crater and hissing through the sky like a dying eagle. First will come the hiss, then the sound of an explosive fire cloud. The heath will illuminate for a moment, long enough for your king to shed an eye on the walking, cannoned machinas which Regan has sent to the fray in this past hour or so.

And the rain rusts it all.

Lear now curls up with a rock. His gilded arm still sticks in its straight position. He looks to it, and gives a silent sob.

"Is man no more than this?" he wails to me, and I say nothing. "Oh, Lear, thou art the thing itself. Unaccommodated man is no more but such a poor, bare, forked animal as thou art... my might is gone."

"We should get him to Regan once more," the Fool says from his bottle. "His wits begin to unsettle again."

"His daughters seek his death," I say. "Canst thou blame him?"

He'd tried to sleep on the airships with Goneril, but Goneril said his soldiers took too much room. He left her for Regan, who drove him out when he demanded to still be called king.

"Oh, Cordelia," he mutters feverishly. "She is gone forever."

And I take my leave for the heath.

The mud sinks into my holed shoes, and the rain pelts down on my sore face. I feel heavy tonight, my friends. Goneril and Regan battle in our blood, and they both lose to the storm.

Only hours ago, Lear was chased from Regan's hands. We escaped, barely with our lives. His baubles he refused to leave in the mud and they weighed us down, but we took them all the same, for he is our king. The old Fool and I tried to keep him between us, but he ran ahead and shouted to the winds, "Blow and crack your cheeks! Rage! Blow! Here I stand, your slave!"

He trudged along, knee-deep in sludge. The battle all round us. "Who's there?" he whispered to us men who kept him between us.

"That's a wise man and a fool," the Fool said quietly, and we kept on until finding the cave.

The king laughed. "My wits begin to turn. Oh that way madness lies…"

The frigid howling of another eagle shot down bursts into a thousand licks of flame only a few stone-throws from where I now stand. My own armor was lost on the heath, and now I am here only with the protection of my tunic and britches. I take a shallow, heated breath on my hands so I can continue to write to you.

But here comes another through the burning, dying heath.

A boy? This boy is no larger than my calf. He hides himself in dark leather clotted with mud and earth. But his lantern waves the faintest light in the din of the darkness. And this is how I spotted him.

"Ho!" I sound out, and he looks to me. "What are you doing on this battleground? Are you of Goneril or Regan?"

"Neither!" the boy howls over the whirring of the walking gears in the distance. The thunder claps above. "And who are you of?"

"Lear!" I say with no cowardice. "Do I shoot you now or let you come closer?"

"Closer, I hope!"

"Then who are you of?"

"Cordelia!" the boy says. "She has a message for our king!"

Our king, he says! Our king, my friends!

"What is the message then?"

The boy scrambles closer to my sitting place, just as a terrible canister falls from the clouds above. It lands at the feet of the walking machinas, and I hear the slithering of gas breathe out. There, unseen, I smell the putrid death scent.

"Hold your mouth!" I shout, and I'm to my feet with my mask round my face. The boy takes his own from his pockets, and I rush to him as the walking machinas fall to the ground. Screams of men not so well equipped are heard in the blind rush of thunder.

I scoop the boy into my arms and flee further away, up the jagged rocks of the heath. Higher grounds–

"Thank you," he shudders through his mask. And we turn to look down below.

It is now full battle.

"Cordelia says she waits in Dover," the boy whispers to me. "She has all of Gaul with her. She wishes to see the kingdom returned to our king."

I watch him, then the airships crash and the machinas fall.

"She returns for Lear then?" I say.

"Aye," the boy says.

I nod and remove my pocket watch from my tunic. I hand it to him. "Tell her that her good friend Kent promises Lear will arrive."

"Aye," the boy says. He takes the pocket watch and stuffs it into his muddy garments. "Then I–" a bomb explodes the heath. "I shall seek another route than from whence I came."

And then he is gone.

The Fool greets me at the door, near to spent. Lear wakes from his small sleep, his glassy eyes in wonderment.

"Who calls?" he whispers.

"A Fool," the Fool says. "A Fool to lead the madman."

I kneel down. I take his ungilded hand in mine. I touch it, the old wrinkled, imperfect skin. It is here I remember shaking hands with my friend when I first arrived in London, long before the gilded arm was set. I touch his sunken cheek, and it's here I remember our kingdom years ago when I first saw the heath in spring's green.

And I see Lear's soft expression return, and it's here where I see hidden the happiest day when he held his youngest for the first time.

"Your Majesty," I say to him. "Your daughter returns for you in Dover."

He looks to me. "Cordelia?"

"Aye," I say.

And quietly, he presses his hand upon my face. "But I banished her. Along with Kent."

"Kent arrives as well," I say. "Cordelia and Kent stand beside you."

"But wherefore do they find reason?" Lear mutters. "I gave them not my kingdom. I gave them not my kind words."

I embrace my king–our king–and although you may disagree with my embrace, I give it. And the old king grows warm once more.

My mother once warned if I did not mind my manners, I would find my end in hell. And there in hell, I would only have madmen to serve.

But soon the water will recede. The gas will clear. The boy will find his way. The airships will fall. The walking cannons will cease to steam. Tintern Abbey will once again be seen to the west, and Cordelia's army will come from the east.

I am to be here. And so I stay. I stay to see the might of King Lear's legacy bring back the heath from rust. It is then, my fellow countrymen, you shall hear this tale and know the true might of a king who fashions a wonder such as Cordelia.

"Devouring Time, rust thou the robot's gears"
by Olivia Waite

Devouring Time, rust thou the robot's gears
And let his copper armor plates grow thin,
Crack the clear glass in the goggle lenses' sphere
And burn the gas in every zeppelin.
Make mad and monstrous creatures drop and die,
And do whate'er thou wilt, unhinging Time
To each mechanic bee and clockwork fly:
But I forbid thee biologic crime.
O keep my living love forever quick,
Nor wear out organs, muscles, heart or brain,
Let her be always vital, never sick,
And let her perfect beauty never wane.
Yet do thy worst, rude Time: should she pass on,
I'll translate her to an automaton.

Measure For Steel-Sprung Measure
by Rebecca Fraimow

Claudio rose at his sister's arrival, coming to the door of his prison cell to grasp Isabella's hands. His were cold, though damp with nervousness—as hers were too, but if this gave him cause for anxiety he showed no sign. There was nothing in her brother's eyes but naked hope. "Now, sister, what's the comfort?"

She had to swallow the lump in her throat before she could speak. He had never really believed that Lord Angelo, the duke's mere deputy, would demand the strictest possible sentence for a crime that until recently had been condemned only by priests and not by civil law. It would be hard for him; she must guide him through it. "Why," she told him, "as all comforts are, most good—most good indeed. Lord Angelo, but thinking on your soul, intends to part it from its stained garb. It shall be habited more brightly hence."

Claudio stared at her, dumb. Perhaps he did not understand. "Therefore," she went on, gently, "your best appointment make with speed. Tomorrow, it is done."

Tomorrow—it was swift, beyond swift, to make such an adjustment. Isabella, as all novices, had been granted a year to settle her mind and to plan the make of her model, choosing the materials and setting the parts by her own hand. Now she felt that the steel-sprung creation that awaited her final vows was more truly Isabella than ever flesh had been. But of course those who took the clockwork habit by sentence rather than by choice were given no say in the make of their soul's future home. Craft was virtue's privilege. A standard golem, factory-hammered iron and clay, was all that awaited the sinner.

Isabella had never had occasion to encounter a clockwork convict, but she had studied the stock blueprints for such in sketching her first designs. Made in assembly, without individuality, it should not have been possible to tell one such golem from another, but it was said that once animated, the featureless faces awakened most marvelously. They still did not look human, oh no, nor in any wise like the men and women they had been. But unique they did look, unique as the spirits that embodied them—truly a soul's habit, as much as any priest's or sister's. The human soul is above all things most wonderful.

She was prepared to tell her brother so, when he was ready to hear it, but for now silence was perhaps best, to let him come to terms. She gripped his hands to give him reassurance and he clutched back. Finally he whispered, "Is there no other remedy?"

"None," she told him firmly, "but such remedy as, to save a head, would cleave a heart in twain."

"But is there *any*?"

He was plaintive as a child. It would be more than cruelty to sentence a child so, never to eat, nor sleep, nor savor any simple, physical joy–but Claudio was not a child anymore. A child could not have committed the act of lewd fornication outside of marriage, could not be held sentence for filling Juliet's belly with child. He was old enough to understand the decisions an adult must make, the values an adult must have. "Yes, brother, you may live," she said, slipping her hands out of his and turning half away. She felt shamed, despite that there was no shame in anything she had done–shamed to be speaking of shameful things with her brother, shamed to admit that the purest things could be tainted. "There is a devilish mercy in the judge, if you'll implore it, that will save your flesh, but fetter you–us both–until our death."

Out of the corner of her eye, she saw Claudio blink. "Perpetual durance?"

"Ay, just–perpetual durance, a restraint, though all the world's vastidity one had, to a determined scope."

"But in what nature?" Claudio seemed as if he was trying to fathom a riddle–as well he might, from her own speech. Why could she not speak straight?

She buried her face in her hands. *Oh, I do fear thee, Claudio,* she thought–amazed to discover in herself it was so. He was her brother; how could she think he would ask of her what she was not willing to give?

But he did not understand her choice to take the habit, had never understood it, and he was young, and foolishly afraid. "I quake," she said aloud–switching to the familiar form, the better to reach him–"lest thou a feverish life should entertain, and all temporal pleasures more respect than a perpetual honor. Darest thou die in body?"

A moment passed, as Claudio worked out that she was, in a roundabout way, calling him a coward, and he reached out to grip her arm. "Why give you me this shame?" he snapped; and now he sounded like an adult, not like the boy of six, and she could breathe. "If this my body is indeed to die, I'll go to meet my fate with a man's daring, though never were I to be man again."

"There spoke my brother," she said, lifting her face. Her cheeks were still red, but the two of them would speak, adult to adult, and she would look him in the eye. She wished fiercely, for the hundredth time, that all this had occurred a week hence; that she had taken her final vows and was safe in her soul's habit, with a sturdy face of porcelain that would not change color no matter with what tempests her heart was battered. "Yes, thou must be sentenced. Thou art too noble to conserve mere life in base corruption. This outward-sainted deputy is a very devil." Her throat was choking up again, with rage and sorrow. "His filth within being cast, he would appear a pond as—as deep as hell!"

"The prenzie Angelo!" Her brother stared at her, shocked, most likely, to hear her use such words. She was shocked at herself. Oh, for the cool of clockwork!

"Oh, 'tis the cunning livery of hell," she said, forcing the words out deliberately this time—for if any did deserve such calling, the hypocrite Lord Angelo did, and to tell this tale to her brother her mouth must be used to foulness. Little matter if it stained her mouth; every part of her body would soon be changed for a better. "Dost thou think, Claudio, that if I might yield unto him my habit, thou might'st be freed?"

"Your habit!" echoed Claudio, in pure amazement.

"Yes." He would not make this leap–the notion was anathema even to think, for a healthy mind. She would have to spell it out for him, though it made her shudder to say it. "He would have it, claiming that to sin on something that is sinless is no sin–and thus to have his sin, and sin again, and sin for all his life and feel no shame. But heavens, he should feel shame! Despising flesh, he contemplates a far worse sin than thine. He'd have my *soul,* my brother, for his lusts. He'd take it from me, and do all he wills–sin on my soul and steal its purity, and all my chance of heaven," and then, to her horror, she began to cry.

Claudio looked as if he had not the least idea what to do. This was no shock; in their childhood, always, it was she who had comforted him. "Thou shalt not do't," he said, weakly, shoving his hands awkwardly against his sides as if searching for a pocket, and a handkerchief, neither of which presented themselves in his rough prison garments.

She rubbed her eyes roughly on her sleeve, her nose likewise, and attempted to take hold of herself. How could anyone regret the loss of a body of flesh, all subject to such frailty! "Were it but my life," she attempted to reassure him, "I'd throw it down for your deliverance as frankly as a pin. Were it but this–this cast of flesh, he'd have it when I left it, and be welcome. But what he asks–"

"Thanks, dear Isabel," said Claudio, cutting her off. His voice now sounded flat, and his hand dropped from her arm.

She did not know what to say after that. "Wouldst have me help thee, Claudio," she asked, finally, "accustom thyself to thy soul's new lodgings? There's teachings I could bring thee, from the sisters—the ways to teach the spirit not to hunger, nor after food, nor drink, nor touch, nor sleep, nor all the thousand natural fooleries that flesh is heir to."

Perhaps that had been a mistake, for at each listing Claudio flinched. "Thanks, Isabel," he said again, and then, "Lord Angelo—"

"What?"

Claudio shook his head. "My mind is 'mazed. He's well known for his wisdom."

"The wisdom of a serpent," said Isabella, bitterly. She had been glad—yes, *glad*—when he had been given command of the city in the Duke's absence. He'd a reputation for virtue unstained, and would make the city virtuous in his image. How then to know that image of perfection was image only? How to know the twisted soul it covered?

"Yet, if 'twere damnable—he being so wise—" He broke off, as if the words were painful to him, and in her heart, she begged him, *say no more.* And yet, if he had pain from his thoughts, still not pain enough to prevent them; the next came out all in a rush. "O Isabel, tell me, what can it harm? 'Tis not the solid flesh on which he'd sin, but on a thing of steel and wire, no more. There's nothing that you'd feel—tell me, with this, who does he hurt?"

Isabella stumbled a step back, staring at her brother. "It is my *soul* he hurts!" she lashed out, hoping to see him look down, embarrassed, caught out. He was afraid again, she told herself, only that. Remind him not to play the coward, and all will be well.

But instead he stared her straight on. "To be no longer man—oh, that is fearful."

"And live by sister's shame—oh, that is hateful!"

"Ay, but to die, and then to wake again and feel oneself not human, but *machine*?" There was a loathing in the word that struck her more than a blow might have. "This sensible warm motion to become all gears and cogs, all calculate, designed—ticking away the time that is not life, and forced to labor ceaselessly, sans rest, sans pleasure, sans love—'tis too horrible!" His hands fisted at his sides, flexed, fisted again. "The weariest and most loathed earthly life that age, ache, penury, and imprisonment can lay on nature is paradise to life that liveth not."

She could not understand it; it sickened her to hear it. First Angelo and now her own brother; how did all these men see through a lens so warped? It was well known that only through discarding the flesh and taking the habit of the soul could man or woman escape original sin. All weakness left behind, all petty nuisance, all that one had not asked for in being born to this sorrowful world—clockwork was life perfected, utter control of the body, utter distillation of the mind. That those who would willingly abandon the normal life of man to attain such perfection were rare, she had known already; that it required sacrifice at first, she had known also—but that any could regard it with such *horror*...

"Alas," she murmured, "alas," for she knew what would come next.

"Sweet sister–" Claudio dropped to his knees, fumbled for her hand. "Let me live. Give up your clockwork form to Angelo. I know you think it sin upon your soul, but it would be an act truly unselfish, which makes of it a virtue–not a sin."

"O faithless coward," said Isabella, blankly. It was harsh, harsher than she meant. But shame was the only tool she could think to use against him now.

And, she had to admit, there was anger blazing in her (for now, still-beating) heart, kindled low but rising. Easy for him to say there was no harm in Angelo's touch upon her crafted form. Easy for him to say. He'd the boy's experience of the flesh. He was a man, and until sin-obsessed Angelo's harsh sentence came upon him, all the power in this city had been his by birthright. He knew *nothing* of what it meant to feel one's body was not one's own. And perhaps it was no bad thing that he learn–for how else would he ever come to see the true and gleaming value of the soul?

"Mercy to thee would prove thyself a bawd," she told him, and turned her back on him, deliberately. "'Tis best thou transmutes quickly."

"O, hear me, Isabella!" pleaded her brother, but she was already walking out the door.

"Where art thou Muse that forget'st me so long?"
by Tucker Cummings

Where art thou Muse that forget'st me so long?
Thy true servant, artificer of steam
Once known abroad for dirigibles strong
Lives off residuals from youthful dreams.
Return forgetful Muse, and straight redeem
This piteous old tinker man of Kent.
No longer content to coast on rusty esteem
I must needs find a new contraption to invent.
Resting Muse, my vacant workshop survey.
O, ennervate my useless, worn down mind!
Release to me a steam-schema today
Before my aging mind's gear springs unwind.
Give my device fame, fast as Time wastes life,
So it and I outlast death's crooked knife.

The Malefaction of Tybalt's Mechanical Armature
by Tim Kane

Tybalt's left hand prickled.

He blocked out the sensation and gripped the pickaxe tighter. Swung it. The metal tip clanked against the rock wall. A bone-rattling tremor shot up his right arm and into his teeth.

The air in the mine clung to his dark skin like a sticky sheet. His breathing came in a ragged pant. He tipped up his cap and mopped the accumulated sweat.

Another itch, this time where the left elbow should have been. He couldn't suppress a glance. The machine puffed a steady stream of oily smoke, forcing the gears to mesh. The pneumatics squeezed the fingers around the shaft of the pickaxe.

This was all that remained of his left arm.

A mechanism.

He licked lips tasting of salt. Gripping the tool again with his callused right hand, he hefted the pickaxe over one shoulder. The machine followed suit. The leather straps that held the mechanical armature in place pulled taut across his chest.

The muscles in his right arm tensed, anticipating the blow. In his left, gears continued to clack together, awaiting the twitch from the stump thrust into the metal contraption.

He heaved forward again, throwing too much into this blow. The metal tip sparked along the mine wall. His muscles screamed and the impact sent shockwaves through his skeleton.

A bell rang, signaling the end of work.

His right hand loosened on the wooden shaft, yet the brass fingers continued to clasp the tool. He had to reach over and pry them away from the pickaxe.

Tybalt emerged from the mine to see the sky melting into a dull purple sludge. The other miners clustered together in the growing gloom, rolling cigarettes. He felt their gazes inch along his mechanical arm. The brass fittings still shone in the dwindling light.

"What ho!" shouted Eckles, the red-haired Irishman. The man never knew when to shut up. "You got oily fountains issuing from your veins."

Tybalt didn't turn to look, but stopped all the same.

Eckles chuckled and separated from the group. The other miners were Irish or German. The grime that coated their bodies would wash away to reveal pale skin. Not so with Tybalt. His arm wasn't the only thing that set him apart.

Eckles pointed toward town.

"Look and see. They is coming for you, boy."

Tybalt glanced at the town, but saw only the shadowy outlines of buildings.

Eckles folded his arms, waiting for a response. After a moment, he added, "Mr. Capulet don't own all of Kansas."

Tybalt spun about and marched toward the man.

Eckles's facade faltered and he stumbled toward the security of the group. The man was scrawny and Tybalt had forty pounds on him.

The mechanical arm hiccuped and sputtered, drawing Eckles's attention. The smoke issuing from the contraption had thinned to a thread. The man couldn't know that the machine hardly had the power now to grasp a bottle.

Tybalt clenched the mechanical fingers, smiling as he saw Eckles's eyes focusing on the movement. "You'll find me ready."

"Seal up your mouth," Eckles said, yet stayed surrounded by the other miners.

Tybalt turned his back to them. As he walked toward town, through a landscape that looked near black in the dying sunlight, he could hear the miners chattering softly.

He wanted to hole up in his room. The spring shaft had unwound, and the pneumatic fluid needed topping off. The plate connecting the armature to his stump smoldered. If not allowed to cool, it would soon sear his skin.

He should unhook the damned thing. Have Mr. Capulet work it over in his machine shop. But Tybalt had never once removed the mechanical arm. It was part of him now.

The twin lines of squat buildings were lit now, lamps blazing against the shadow of night.

He felt that phantom twinge again in his left arm. This time, the palm itched.

With his right hand, he gripped a tiny curio hanging around his neck. Wrapped in twine, it consisted of a bone from the pinky finger of his severed hand. The thing was supposed to keep the ghostly itching at bay.

It didn't do squat.

He drew closer to the first set of buildings. Light poured from the saloon, along with the clamor of men laughing and whooping. The rest of the miners were sure to take up residence within the hour. It was a Saturday night.

Tybalt aimed toward the end of town and his room at the Verona Hotel. As he passed the saloon, he spied twelve new horses tied up outside. Tucked under one saddle, serving as a horse blanket, was the gray jacket of a Confederate soldier.

He should have continued on. The gears jittered. Soon, the machinations would wind down, leaving the arm as little more than dead metal. Yet he found himself turning toward the saloon. Something about the voices inside pricked his interest.

The wooden planks creaked under his boots. Pushing open the doors, Tybalt scanned the room. In the absence of the miners, the newcomers dominated the establishment. Several sat along the bar, staring contemplatively into glasses of whiskey.

All signs of service had been stripped away. A few wore pistols tucked through their belts, but no other markings or emblems signified that these men were once soldiers in the Confederate army.

Loud guffawing caught Tybalt's attention. Three men occupied the far corner. A bearded fellow held a slender knife between his fingers, hilt up. A second lanky man stood a few feet away. He grinned, displaying a set of crooked teeth.

The bearded man flung the knife. It spun through the air, directly toward the second man's chest.

The lanky man snatched the blade before it struck home. "Dang, Ben," he said, showing off those crooked teeth again. "We must have you dance." He sauntered over, handing the knife back to the bearded Ben. "You throw like a girl."

The third man giggled from the corner. He was in the shadow of the other two.

Tybalt stepped toward the trio.

"Mercutio," Ben said, tapping the lanky man on the shoulder. All three turned toward Tybalt. The one in the corner stood, his face catching the light.

The features had aged in five years–shifting from youth to manhood–but the landmarks remained. The mop of black hair. The round eyes and slender nose. This was Romeo Montague.

A spike of pain lanced through Tybalt's left arm. He felt the metal teeth clamp down on his fingers again, chewing flesh and crushing bone.

Mercutio stepped forward.

"Lord, ain't you a sight? Look at that arm there." He nudged Ben. "Tell me, boy, was your mother a steam locomotive?"

This pulled a grin out of Ben.

Romeo stared at Tybalt, recognition flickering in his eyes.

The mechanical armature hissed as a jet of steam issued through a crack. Tybalt twitched his stump and the fingers grudgingly obeyed, flexing open.

"I declare," Mercutio said, flinging his arms wide and announcing to the entire saloon, "This man is his very own cotton-picking machine."

Ben placed a hand on Mercutio's shoulder. "Let's retire. The hot day has your blood stirring."

Mercutio shrugged away from his his friend. "You would quarrel with a man that had a hair more or less in his beard than you had. You'd quarrel with a man for cracking nuts. And yet you will tutor me about quarreling?"

"All eyes gaze on us," Ben said.

Tybalt forced himself to look around. The conversation had died as the rest of the Confederate soldiers stared at him.

"Men's eyes were meant to look," Mercutio said. "Let them gaze."

Tybalt turned to face Romeo. If hate could burn, then the boy should have blackened to ash that very second.

Romeo stared back. He knew. Had to.

Mercutio stepped directly in front of Tybalt, blocking his view.

"I don't budge for no man's pleasure."

Tybalt swiveled and marched toward the door.

Mercutio leaned against Ben and began to sing. "An old hare hoar, and an old hare hoar, is very good meat in Lent."

Tybalt continued for the door. Sweat beaded along his forehead, not the product of physical labor but of inner turmoil. His right arm quivered. He squeezed the hand into a fist, the fingernails digging into the palm and drawing blood.

As Tybalt pushed open the door, Mercutio's voice shot up, almost to a shout. "But a hare that is hoar is too much for a score, when it hoars ere it be spent."

The cool night air washed over Tybalt's skin, chilling the layer of sweat. He veered to the back of the saloon, and soon the sounds of Mercutio singing became blurred and unintelligible.

He uncurled his fingers, breaking the fist. Blood coated his fingernails and there were four crescent grooves in his palm. He slid his hand into his jacket pocket and located the thin brass tool Capulet had given him. Intended for modest repairs in the field, it was all he had.

He slotted one end into the spring shaft and cranked the tool clockwise. After several rotations, the spring stiffened, storing energy. Tybalt forced it tighter. Blood from his palm dribbled down the metal handle.

Smoke and steam hissed around the bolts as the internal pressure grew. It would have to hold. He couldn't risk leaving now. Not after so long.

His mind zeroed in on Romeo. He remembered the boy's smooth hands on the cotton gin's crank. Romeo was one of the owner's sons, a Montague. The boy typically remained in the manor house, but that day, something had drawn him out. The machine churned away, threshing cotton, with the boy's hands only loosely on the crank. Romeo gazed across the field at Juliet. Tybalt stiffened. The boy dared stare at his cousin that way.

Tybalt had hefted another bunch of cotton and shoved into the machine. The sawtoothed cylinder chewed up the plants. Then Romeo spun the crank too hard. The machine sputtered and Tybalt's hand slipped. Red spattered the cotton, creating tiny crimson clouds. Tybalt screamed loud enough for the entire Montague plantation to hear.

Perhaps an hour passed before the rest of the miners arrived, amplifying the ruckus in the saloon. Tybalt stayed in the shadows, his mechanical gears clicking away. His stomach clenched, but this was secondary to his arm. He continued to ratchet the spring shaft, building the tension.

The moon rose, overseeing the town like a massive eye and pouring a sickly yellow glow over everything.

Gradually, men trickled out, each progressively more tipsy and ungainly. The miners, having less coin to spend, were the first to leave. Then clusters of Confederates staggered down the street toward the Verona Hotel at the far end of town.

Tybalt searched each face lit by the sallow moonlight. None were Romeo's.

The plate against the stump of his left arm seared under the internal barrage of steam. He vented some of the gas, but could only risk a little. Too much and the gears would grind to a halt. He had to cope with the pain.

Still he waited.

Then the trio emerged. The bearded one, Ben, staggered into a support beam. The lankier Mercutio followed, a bottle clutched in one hand.

Finally Romeo. The boy teetered less than the

others, his feet finding their way down to the street without falter.

Mercutio giggled—a toothy grin affixed to his face. "If love is rough with you, be rough with love."

He took a step forward, slipped, and tumbled down. Whiskey drained into the street, turning the dirt to pulpy muck.

Romeo and Ben stared at Mercutio, each doubling over in laughter.

Tybalt stepped forward. His arm whirred and clicked. Romeo had his back to the saloon.

"Turn," Tybalt said.

Romeo staggered around as Tybalt closed the distance. He raised his left arm, curling the mechanical fingers into a fist. The bone curio bounced along his neck.

"Look upon your death."

Romeo's eyes widened as Tybalt brought the arm down. No pickaxe clasped there. Instead, the spring shaft released its tension on the young man's shoulder.

Bone cracked and the boy crumbled to the dirt. Romeo shrieked, gripping the wounded shoulder.

The armature stiffened from the impact, its gears sputtering nearly to a stop.

"Hold off," Ben shouted. He'd pulled a blackened pistol from somewhere and now aimed it at Tybalt's head. "I do but keep the peace."

"What? Drawn and talk of peace?" Tybalt spat in the dirt.

Romeo scrabbled across the street, whimpering with the effort.

"I hate the word," Tybalt said. "As I hate hell, all

Montagues, and you." Blood thumped in his ears. His phantom arm crackled with sensation.

He looked Ben straight on. "Shoot, coward."

Ben extended the pistol. Then he pulled the trigger. The gun exploded in a bang of black powder. The man fell to the ground, gripping his eyes.

Mercutio lunged forward, filling the space between Tybalt and Romeo. He had unsheathed the knife from earlier.

Tybalt jerked the stump housed in the mechanical armature. The gears spun as if coated in molasses. Still, he managed to bring the arm up.

"Dishonorable. Vile submission." Mercutio wobbled unsteadily on his legs.

"What would you have of me?" Tybalt said.

"Nothing but your life!" Mercutio jabbed forward, but the drink had taken its toll. The blade, meant for Tybalt's gut, instead jammed into the spring shaft of the mechanical arm.

Tybalt twisted his body and the weapon slipped from the man's hand, now lodged in the metal spring. He forced the armature up, ugly black smoke puffing out now, and clamped the fingers around the lanky man's throat. Then Tybalt squeezed. Mercutio's cry came out as a raspy gurgle.

Romeo staggered to his feet, wincing. He rushed forward and clasped the mechanical arm, grunting as he pushed.

Tybalt gripped the knife and pried it from the mechanics. The boy was right there, inches away. He thrust the blade forward. Romeo wrangled with the armature, shifting his body to the side. The knife missed, but found a home in Mercutio's chest. Tybalt released his grip.

A dark blob grew along Mercutio's shirt. He staggered, staring at the knife in his chest. It quivered with each passing heartbeat.

"A scratch. A scratch. But good enough." Mercutio slumped onto the dirt street and the boy knelt beside him. "Why the devil did you come between us?" Mercutio's voice was a harsh whisper. "I was hurt under your arm." His once-white shirt was completely stained. It looked black under the yellow moonlight.

He glanced at Tybalt. "A plague on both of you." He clenched his teeth, his chest heaving, and then he spat up blood. A wry smile crossed his lips. "You've made worms' meat of me."

His body went still.

Tybalt stood, watching. Black oil poured over the brass fittings, bubbling with the internal heat of the machine. His skin burned where the leather straps held the machination against his body. The gears spun down to a stop. The arm was a dead thing now, its mission yet to be accomplished.

Romeo spun around, eyes blazing.

"Mercutio's soul is but a little way above our heads."

"Wretched boy," Tybalt said. "You brought him here. Now go follow him."

"This will determine that," Romeo cried, launching forward.

The two fell backward onto the street. The boy's hands, slick with Mercutio's blood, groped for the throat. Tybalt forced his right arm in between and shoved the boy off.

Romeo tumbled to the street, but quickly found his footing again. He right arm moved with a painful jerk, the shoulder dislocated.

Tybalt lurched to his feet, but the armature weighed him down. Now unmoving, the thing felt heavier than before. He huffed and wheezed.

Romeo charged, slamming Tybalt against a railing. His fingers again sought the man's throat. "Either you or I shall die this day."

Tybalt placed his hand over the boy's face, meaning to push him back. Then Romeo's fingers caught the leather strap that secured the machination. He worked at the buckle.

Tybalt felt the plate against his stump shift. His burned skin roiled with pain. He could not lose his arm. Not twice to the same man. He clamped his hand down over Romeo's, attempting to pry the fingers loose, but the boy persisted, moonlight glinting in his eyes.

With a grimace, Romeo brought his wounded right arm up, and his two hands prevailed against Tybalt's one, unfastening the buckle. The weight of armature pulled it down. Skin, fused to the metal by the heat, tore away with it. Blood bubbled out in rivulets, the liquid sizzling when it struck the overheated machine.

Tybalt screamed, clasping at the fallen armature with his right hand. He gripped the metal, scalding his fingers, and managed to heft the thing back over his stump.

Romeo gripped the machination with both his hands. Hauled it completely off.

Tybalt fell into the dirt street. Tears filled his eyes.

He stared at the mechanical armature, now in Romeo's grasp.

"Give it back," he said, his voice thin and hard.

Romeo stared at the machine, the metal scorching his fingers. Gears absently whirled as steam hissed from its cracks. Once gleaming, the brass fittings were blackened with oil and soot.

It looked nothing like an arm.

Romeo dropped it. The hunk of brass and gears kicked up dust as it landed. He swiveled and hurried to Ben, who still clasped a hand over his eyes.

Blood gushed from Tybalt's stump, puddling in the dirt. He scrambled toward the abandoned machine. He gripped the blackened metal and shoved it over his stump. His whole body clenched as hot metal met flesh. Teeth clamped shut against the pain, he cinched the strap and threaded the buckle.

Blood continued to trickle, winding its way along the spring shaft and gears, mixing with the grease and soot. Tybalt willed his legs to work. Hate propelled his body up, but his heart throbbed heavily in his chest.

Romeo had managed to get Ben onto a horse. He turned to face Tybalt. His gaze took in the blood-soaked machine.

Tybalt's legs gave way, and he fell to his knees. He gasped for breath, a stab of pain accompanying each contraction of his lungs. He surged forward, gripping Romeo's pant leg with his right hand.

The boy stepped back, and Tybalt fell into the street.

"Here," Romeo said. "Here you will remain. With the worms."

Tybalt's fingers groped for the boy, now out of reach. His face lay in the dirt. Each ragged breath kicking up sprays of dust.

Romeo led the horse and Ben down the street.

The blackened metal of the dead arm cracked as steam found its way to freedom. The machine shuddered, popping loose two bolts. Steam surged, then tapered off. Broken gears twirled mindlessly, spun by the escaping gas.

Tybalt's heart thumped hard, but the space between each beat grew longer. Blackness swirled his vision. He saw Romeo's distant form, moving farther away.

The venting steam dwindled down to whisper. The metal popped and clicked, cooling. The machination fell into a gentle slumber, its energy spent.

Tybalt slept with it. The two falling into stillness as one.

"Not from the stars do I my judgement pluck"
by J.H. Ashbee

Not from the stars do I my judgement pluck,
'Cause my machine usurps astronomy;
And though I tell of good or evil luck,
Undead, dust-storms, of regimes' quality;
Though I can fortune's best enigmas' crack
'Pointing each to his 'ther, rain and wind,
Or warn airship crew of pirates' attack,
By sharing forth what my machine doth find.
But in thine eyes no knowledge I derive;
Though eyes are portals to innermost art,
Twelve hundred steam engines could not connive
To pump all the bilge from your brain and heart.
So thus of thee this I prognosticate:
Thy end is truth's and beauty's joy and fate!

Julius C-ZR
by Bret Jones

The noise overwhelmed the forum as shouts echoed and raised to the heavens. Fervor struck a chord, and that chord reverberated into celebration, and that in turn, to a near maelstrom of outpouring. Brutus leaned against a pillar in the midst of the throng witnessing the frenzy. It made him ill.

The airship buzzed rhythmically in the skies, parting the puffy white cloud encircling it like something sent from the gods. Silvery fins burnished bright as the sun reflected off the polished metal. Brutus choked back bile. Wanting to blame it on the over-ripe fruit he had eaten for his breakfast, he knew better. The C-ZR, the model approved by the Senate itself, chewed up the open sky in his airship—also Senate approved!

An officer shooed the mechanicals off the street. A tightly wound carpenter and other steam-driven menial laborers purred into the alleyways that connected to the forum. With half their brains replaced with cogs and whirling wheels, the mechanicals still possessed human curiosity and questions, but the (again!) Senate approved steam-pressurized cerebral implants overrode these urges, pushing the workers back to their appointed tasks. Pulsing steam pressure puffed quietly as the mechanicals scampered off the main thoroughfare.

Brutus followed them with his gaze as the air giant blotted out part of the sun, casting a malignant shadow over the Romans below. How much had the monstrosity cost the citizenry? But on a whim, C-ZR demanded the transport.

"He will grace all of Rome now with his presence," Brutus mumbled to no one but himself. He wasn't sure of his sentiments being acknowledged or supported by the maddening crowd. And, on top of that, a C-ZR-sponsored air race would soon follow to appease the sport-deprived (that was a laugh!) citizens. Brutus saw Cassius bearing down on one of his servants across the forum. He waved, but to no avail. He didn't bother yelling, either, because of the cacophony of sound.

The airship hovered above the forum. The buzz from the rotors turned into a deadly hum as the blades sheared the air. Smaller airships eased into position near the now "royal" airship. Since when did the term "royal" apply to a C-ZR, thought Brutus. Once upon an age, royalty applied to the Queen of Egypt, not to a Roman.

We are in the midst of something ugly.

The racers positioned in a straight formation, ready for *Julius*, the newly built C-ZR, to start them off on their race to Neapolis. Brutus grumbled about the cost of such luxury. This had not been Senate approved! In point of fact, C-ZR used his self-appointed position to bypass any Senate interference.

"Brutus!" he heard from across the forum, but only

just. Cassius pointed to a spot on the opposite side of the steps, nearly cleared for C-ZR's entrance. Word spread that Calphurnia, his wife, would be with him today. Poor, barren Calphurnia, thought Brutus. And with this version of C-ZR, she wouldn't see children. Brutus fought the crowds to get to Cassius. It proved more difficult than he thought.

A booming, mechanically enhanced voice shouted: "Calphurnia!"

"Peace, ho! C-ZR speaks." Brutus heard the grating voice of Casca, an "oil-pumper" to C-ZR. Casca hadn't heard this contemptuous nickname, as it signified that his only function was to lubricate C-ZR's joints and feed more fuel into the steam engine that powered his frame and nearly all his mind. But to Brutus, it suited the self-serving Senator well.

C-ZR again yelled, "Calphurnia!" His thick arm reached through the crowd and pulled her back. The flyers sped past, hovering near rope ladders, ready for C-ZR's signal to start the race.

"Here, my lord," she said. Deep crevices in her face spoke to the misery she must have felt with the "new" version of her husband. For appearances' sake, she gripped C-ZR's metal arm as a show to the people of their union.

"Stand you directly in Antonius' way when he doth run his course–Antonius!"

Another "oil-pumper" toadied up to the great man/machine. A puff of white steam billowed from the base of his neck, wafting into the sky above him. And to think that Brutus once admired Marc Antony as a voice of the people.

"C-ZR, my lord." Brutus stood near enough to smell the burnt fuel coming off of him. He swallowed back more bile.

C-ZR pointed to his wife as he spoke to Antonius. "Forget not in your speed, Antonius, to touch Calphurnia, for our elders say the barren, touched in this holy chase, shake off their sterile curse."

There it was—talk of children! Brutus saw Cassius flinch as well. A grimace grew into conspiracy, Brutus well knew. Better to keep his thoughts just that— thoughts.

He saw Calpurnia's gaunt face blush, not in embarrassment, but shame. Once the beauty of Rome, she held the eye of every Senator until Julius claimed her for his own. With three miscarriages, the last one rendering her barren, Calpurnia appeared emaciated, a ghost of her former self.

"I shall remember," Antonius answered. "When C-ZR says, 'do this,' it is performed."

"Set on, and leave no ceremony out."

Antonius bowed before C-ZR and signaled his skipper, who hastened to enter into his airship, *The Starling*, thus named by Julius himself for the black fins cast into the side of the powerful vehicle. Once belonging to the people, the powerful airship could now be seen moored near Antony's palace.

As Brutus skirted through the throng, avoiding C-ZR's gaze, a great shout came from the pressing swarm of bodies. At first it sounded like the cries of someone committed to the outskirts of the city because of madness, or a mechanical whose cogs spun out of alignment with no chance of repair. Such was the frenzy that C-ZR now commanded of the citizenry.

"C-ZR!" The voice sounded furious, even deadly amongst the throng of onlookers.

"Ha! Who calls?" C-ZR asked no one in particular. He knew someone would answer.

A man pulling himself along the base of the steps crawled forward. Brutus noted the man's missing legs and his amputated fist where a whirring of gears that resembled fingers had been bolted.

Casca waved his arms to get the attention of the crowd, the flyers, and the makeshift band that scraped on homemade instruments. He formed his hands into a trumpet of flesh.

"Bid every noise be still! Peace yet again!" he screamed above the din.

C-ZR came forward, a gear interlocking with another which focused his left eye downward to the step. Pressurized steam escaped a small portal near his left ear.

"Who is it in the press that calls on me? I hear a tongue, shriller than all the music, cry 'C-ZR!'–Speak. C-ZR is turned to hear." The silence that followed his command moved in waves throughout the crowd. Within a matter of seconds quiet filled the forum.

"Beware the ides of March," the man said, obviously a seer of things to come. Brutus caught a quick glimpse of Cassius grinning. Beyond mischief, it portended doom.

"What man is that?" C-ZR inquired suddenly–and of Brutus.

The great Senator fluttered out a response: "A soothsayer bids you beware the ides of March."

"Set him before me. Let me see his face."

Cassius eagerly entered the scene, glee flushing in his crimson cheeks. He came down to the legless man. "Fellow, come from the throng. Look upon C-ZR."

C-ZR's cog-driven eye readjusted itself. Another puff of steam escaped the hatch. Brutus chided himself at the thought of driving a blade into that exhaust port in hopes ending his C-ZR's lifespan. He knew it wouldn't work. Designers of the C-ZR model saw to that.

The seer used his steel fingers to grip onto the lip of the next step. Gasping, he pulled himself up toward the leader of all the Romans, the leader of half the known world. He sucked air deeply into his lungs. His journey covered many leagues, that much was obvious.

"What sayst thou to me now? Speak once again," C-ZR ordered the pathetic creature at his feet.

"Beware the ides of March," he repeated. The crowd murmured at the audacity of the man.

All eyes fell on C-ZR. His eye readjusted again, this time on the crowd of followers. He knew a political opportunity when he saw one. "He is a dreamer. Let us leave him. Pass!"

The seer bowed his head down to the step. The throng erupted as C-ZR pointed to the flock of airships floating in the clouds. C-ZR reached for Calphurnia and raced toward the newly constructed platform, where he would signal the beginning of the race. The pack of pressed bodies surged forward after him leaving Brutus and Cassius to themselves on the steps. Even the seer, realizing his failed attempt to warn C-ZR, crept behind the departed citizens.

"Will you go see the order of the course?" Cassius

asked. He brushed dust off of the piston that powered his amputated arm, yet another casualty in a C-ZR-sponsored campaign. Brutus thanked what gods looked after him that he still possessed all his original limbs. The others, torn and wounded, thanked Vejovis, who brought the power of healing steam to the descendents of Romulus and Remus. Brutus slit a goat's throat annually to show his appreciation for the gift to the people, but it also passing over him. The steam-powered metal extended life and gave power, but it also devoured the soul of the altered man and none of the mechanizers could understand it, much less repair the error.

But none would stand against the power of the gods, or the strength of the military that stood firmly behind C-ZR.

"Not I," he said quietly.

"I pray you, do."

He gazed at Cassius, wondering at his sincerity, or lack thereof. "I am not gamesome. I do lack some part of that quick spirit that is in Antony. Let me not hinder, Cassius, your desires. I'll leave you." As he spun on his heel to return home, a piston hissed behind him. He felt Cassius' hand grab at his tunic.

"Brutus, I do observe you now of late I have not from your eyes that gentleness and show of love as I was wont to have. You bear too stubborn and too strange a hand over your friend that loves you." A gear clicked against another, retracting Cassius' hand. The pain of the prosthetic showed clearly on his face. Brutus knew the story. Cassius, filled with patriotic fervor, dove after C-ZR in the Rubicon. On the other side, he fought fiercely, bravely, even. But his flesh became subject to a cannon-blade, a steam-powered monstrosity that nearly defeated their popular leader.

Brutus opened his mouth to speak, but the tiniest cheer hailed in the distance. The airships maneuvered into position during their conversation. Now the machines of either transportation, or death, as C-ZR demonstrated, puttered toward the horizon.

"Cassius, be not deceived. If I have veiled my look, I turn the trouble of my countenance merely upon myself. Vexed I am of late with passions of some difference, conceptions only proper to myself, which give some soil perhaps to my behaviors." He wanted to continue, the thoughts were there, but nothing came out of his mouth. Another distant shout caught his attention.

"Then, Brutus, I have much mistook your passion, by means whereof this breast of mine hath buried thoughts of great value, worthy cogitations. Tell me, good Brutus, can you see your face?"

With his human hand, Cassius gently steered him toward his auto-chariot. A steady coughing of white-tinted steam burped from a pipe set below one of the metal inlaid wheels. Cassius released a lever attached to the engine conveniently anchored to the outer hull of the chariot. It *chug-chugged* forward, away from the crowd that stood gaping at the airships racing off into the blue yonder.

"No, Cassius, for the eye sees not itself but by reflection, by some other things," Brutus answered hurriedly. Although they were brothers-in-law, Brutus guarded himself. He knew that Cassius recently converted to the philosophy of Epicurus, which Brutus didn't feel sure of, as the Greek's ideas did not fit with Rome's steam-powered vision of the future.

As the auto-chariot sputtered through the empty streets of Rome, their conversation turned to things more conspiratorial. Brutus guarded his tongue as well as his tone. Cassius did not. Every word he uttered pushed and prodded Brutus nearer to the precipice. An observer of his fellow man, Cassius read the division in Brutus' mind.

"Into what dangers would you lead me, Cassius," Brutus asked above the chugging of the engine, "that you would have me seek into myself for that which is not in me?" He knew what he was willing to do if it came to it, to rid Rome of C-ZR, but he daren't reveal a fraction of that to Cassius. An idle word could be misconstrued as open rebellion, which he labored against in his heart every day. Beneath it all, Brutus still valued C-ZR's leadership and authority. But what cost to Rome?

A shout rang out through the streets over Cassius speaking empty words to him. "Had he not heard?" he thought Cassius hissed. He couldn't be certain for the shouting behind them. "Brutus," Cassius barked, "be prepared to hear."

Another shout of the people surged through the cobble-stoned streets.

"What means this shouting?" Brutus blurted. "I do fear the people choose C-ZR for their king." He regretted saying it the moment the words came out of his mouth. A spark of light beamed on Cassius' prosthetic as he pulled a lever causing the auto-chariot to change course.

"Ay, do you fear it? Then must I think you would not have it so," Cassius said.

"I would not, Cassius. Yet I love him well." That he knew to be true without politics, motive, or play for power. Julius without the C-ZR component did great things, not just for Brutus, but for all Rome.

The auto-chariot sputtered forth down a wider street toward familiar surroundings. Cassius guided them to the Curia Julia, the seat of the Roman Senate. Brutus felt the pressure of its authority and center of Roman life. The Republic offered a civilized way to govern the people, but now what did it have to give its citizens? C-ZR declared himself ruler for life, which could mean generations as the steam-powered additions prolonged his lifespan.

Brutus grabbed at his brother-in-law's cold, dead arm. "Thou knowest things pure and good, Cassius. Gaul and the Rubicon make this seem just and right to the people for glory's sake. And for thy part, too, was such power made. His soul nearly departed its white husk with blood caked on his face and his body. Then wisdom struck like a forge's hammer as the Senate made him a new creature. This C-ZR born from Vulcan's steam power. His mind no more than a box of mere coal. The heart within his breast no longer flesh but a beating, pulsing thing of iron."

"I was born free as C-ZR. So were you. We both have fed as well, and we can both endure the winter's cold as well as he," Cassius retorted. "C-ZR is still man inside the metal we made from the mind of the gods' power. Such power is not for one man alone. Thou hast the courage to see as few can."

Cassius steered the chariot outside the Curia. He shot a lever into place and the engine idled back. Without looking back, he thrust himself from the chariot into the hallowed walls of the seat of government. Brutus reluctantly followed.

Cassius took a seat on one of the stone benches facing the orator's area down below. He waved at the structure that held them both in its invisible grip. "For once upon a raw and gusty day, the troubled Tiber chafing with her shores, C-ZR said to me, 'Darest thou, Cassius, now leap in with me into this angry flood and swim to yonder point?'" Cassius scoffed at the memory. He stood up and raised his voice making sure the echo would reverberate all around them. "Upon the word, accoutred as I was, I plungèd in and bade him follow. So indeed he did. The torrent roared, and we did buffet it with lusty sinews, throwing it aside and stemming it with hearts of controversy. But ere we could arrive the point proposed, C-ZR cried, 'Help me, Cassius, or I sink!' I, as Aeneas, our great ancestor, did from the flames of Troy upon his shoulder the old Anchises bear, so from the waves of Tiber did I the tired C-ZR." He strode to the center of the orator's area.

"I still love him and will not speak treason," Brutus responded softly, almost too quiet for Cassius to hear. He was of two minds and could not commit to either.

"And this man is now become a god, and Cassius is a wretched creature and must bend his body if C-ZR carelessly but nod on him," Cassius spat. His face flushed and his arm energized with steam power ready to compensate for any action to be taken. He thrust his arm into a portal of the metal pillar fixed to the dais. A burst of steam exited the exhaust portals beneath his feet. A grainy image appeared above the stone floor near the first tier of benches.

"He had a fever when he was in Spain," Cassius said as he narrated the action playing out before Brutus from the hologram. Cassius pointed with his good arm at the images his appendage recorded. "And when the fit was on him, I did mark how he did shake. 'Tis true, this god did shake! His coward lips did from their color fly, and that same eye whose bend doth awe the world did lose his luster."

Brutus watched with fixed eyes as shimmering versions of C-ZR and Cassius played out before him. Just like a scene from the theatre so popular in Rome, Brutus stood mesmerized. He tried to read the lips of both men as the image flickered with no sound. The pain and frustration played on both men's face. The scene vanished replaced by another where C-ZR lay on a mountain of animal skins in a tent.

"I did hear him groan," Cassius continued his narration. "Ay, and that tongue of his that bade the Romans mark him and write his speeches in their books–'Alas,' it cried, 'give me some drink, Titinius,' as a sick girl. Ye gods, it doth amaze me a man of such a feeble temper should so get the start of the majestic world and bear the palm alone." Brutus watched, transfixed to the spinning pictures near the foot of the dais.

Another shout thundered against the walls. Ignoring the playback, Brutus ran to an opening in the Curia and glared into the air and watched the airships fade away, into mere shadows of specks against the face of the sun. "Another general shout! I do believe that these applauses are for some new honors that are heaped on C-ZR." He stood on tip-toe to see more, but couldn't.

Surely they wouldn't make him a king!

Cassius shut off the images looping back to the first replaying scenes already shown. "Why, man, he doth bestride the narrow world like a Colossus, and we petty men walk under his huge legs and peep about to find ourselves dishonorable graves."

Without a word, Brutus pushed away from Cassius and ran from the slit across the stone-cut benches out of the Curia. He leapt on board the auto-chariot, quickly identifying the navigation system. A surge of steam built up pressure, but he hadn't switched the lever to release it into the drive function. It coughed loudly when it released the fiery vapor through its exhaust. Brutus nearly jumped off the uncooperative beast to run down the streets. A sense of panic flowed through him with each cheer from the crowd.

Cassius trotted to his transport and corrected what Brutus had done, sending the auto-chariot back toward the forum. Steam chugged harder through the drive system as Cassius fed it more heat from the tiny engine.

Placing his real hand on Brutus' shoulder, he tried to ease his kinsman's growing dread. Sensing he may have overplayed his hand, he smiled warmly, using a different tack. "Men at some time are masters of their fates," he said just above the hiss of the engine. "The fault, dear Brutus, is not in our stars but in ourselves, that we are underlings. Brutus and C-ZR—what should be in that 'C-ZR'? Why should that name be sounded more than yours? Write them together, yours is as fair a name."

Brutus frowned, but Cassius wouldn't be swayed from his course. "Sound them, it doth become the mouth as well. Weigh them, it is as heavy. Conjure with 'em, 'Brutus' will start a spirit as soon as 'C-ZR.'"

Mouthing "Brutus" softly over and over, Cassius watched as a wave of indecision passed over his comrade's face. He continued on, seeing how his debate caused deep turmoil leading, he hoped, to some brave decision on Brutus' part.

Speaking of Rome's nobility, he reminded his friend of another Brutus: Lucius Junius Brutus, who overthrew a monarchy to establish the Republic. Tears formed in his eyes as he recounted this beloved man—and Brutus' own ancestor. He could see the knife of discord twist deeper in Brutus' heart. Lucius Junius tore down the walls of tyranny; why couldn't his descendant?

"That you do love me, I am nothing jealous. What you would work me to, I have some aim. How I have thought of this and of these times I shall recount hereafter. For this present, I would not, so with love I might entreat you, be any further moved," Brutus said as they approached the forum.

Sensing his moment, Cassius slipped an awl-shank casually into the palm of Brutus's hand. The dreaded device created for the purpose of destroying the U-SPR and M-PR models of half-castes. Two, Cassius had dispatched himself. Brutus touched the wicked tip, thinking that it was this very weapon that had done it. But could it annihilate a C-ZR? The C-ZR design meant to eliminate the deficiency that the awl-shank could puncture in the metal skin grafted to the amalgam of man and steam.

"What you have said, I will consider," Brutus said as his fingertip brushed along the awl-shank. "What you have to say, I will with patience hear, and find a time both meet to hear and answer such high things. Till then, my noble friend, chew upon this: Brutus had rather be a villager than to repute himself a son of Rome under these hard conditions as this time is like to lay upon us."

Another shout tore through the streets.

"Another general shout!" Brutus said.

Cassius spun a lever on the chariot. A cough of pressure escapes the exhaust as it whirls back toward the tumult. A dark smile spread on his scarred face. A feeling of foreboding, perhaps from the gods themselves, filled Brutus.

The chariot careened around a corner, which caused the engine to compensate with a sudden burst of speed. Both men held onto the lip of the chariot basket and onto one another. The awl-shank burned in Brutus's hand with a fire he had not felt before in his life. He understood the full ramifications of Cassius's haunting words. The U-SPR and M-PR models were vicious, yes, but this C-ZR, this *Julius*... his friend...

He opened his mouth to speak, but heard one final shout that he thought would crush them with its power. He chose his words carefully. After all, once a member of the Senate, always a member... and one to always play the diplomat.

Brutus repeated as the engine powered down:

"What you have said, I will consider."

"I am glad that my weak words have struck but thus much show of fire from Brutus," Cassius made haste to say, but he knew Brutus hadn't heard him. He watched as Brutus ran among the citizens to see if C-ZR accepted the laurel of kingship.

Brutus nearly choked on the tyranny of the treason, but he could not bear the thought of tyranny from a self-proclaimed dictator, either. The awl-shank drilled into his skin as he pocketed it away from prying eyes. He loved Julius, but C-ZR turned his stomach. Julius of old stood for all things Roman–justice, fairness, strength, and the Republic.

Cassius eased a lever back against the wheel. The chariot slowed as the engine purred down to an idle. It coughed quietly and stopped. He replenished the tiny engine's fuel supply. When the people dispersed, he would need a quick retreat. With the seeds sown with his brother-in-law, he would need to move swiftly to gather the others disconcerted with C-ZR. If he arrived at Brutus' doorstep with supporters... yes, it would work.

"The games are done and C-ZR is returning," Brutus said as if to no one. He knew Cassius was miles away in his thoughts, by now planning the next step in his awful scheme.

C-ZR, Calphurnia, and a score of Roman citizens poured back into the forum like the flood waters of the Tiber. Brutus caught C-ZR's gear-driven eye glaring all about him. He had seen that look too often, and more so of late. The eye stopped as it fell on Cassius. A grimace passed over C-ZR's face. Calphurnia gripped his arm as if death itself stalked them both. As far as Cassius was concerned, it did. The frenzy of the crowd obviously upset her. An artificial hand gently hissed steam as C-ZR laid it on her shoulder. Again, his eyes whirred with a *f-r-r-r* sound as it focused on Cassius.

"Look you, Cassius, the angry spot doth glow on C-ZR's brow, and all the rest look like a chidden train," Brutus whispered, even though the shouts of the mob muted anything he said. C-ZR carried that same look right before he killed someone. A quick breath passed. In that moment Brutus felt the full brunt of C-ZR's immense power and authority. Wasn't this why he dared carry the awl-shank on his person? Could he do it? Would he?

My dear friend Julius…

Not anymore, only C-ZR remained.

To save Rome he would do anything. Did that mean burrowing with the awl-shank until he found the kill switch on C-ZR? One thrust wouldn't do it, either. He hadn't experienced the kill of an awl-shank like Cassius had, but again, those were on inferior designs. The C-ZR model, gleaming brightly in the sun before him, outclassed the U-SPR and M-PRs. How many thrusts would it take to shut him down?

As if reading his mind, Cassius waved at a Senator, another of their brotherhood who would explain C-ZR's wrath and listen to the growing plot. If only the crowd weren't so congested, thought Cassius, they could end it right here, right now. He chided himself. No. Better to wait with more support from the disgruntled. C-ZR may have whined like a child when sick or nearly drowning, but that didn't mean he lacked strength—and the augmentation amplified it to a degree which no one could even guess.

C-ZR flagged down Antony with his good arm. On cue, Antony in turn signaled two airships hovering nearby. In an instant, steam roared into the engines, lifting ships high above the crowd to act as escort for the despot. Calphurnia stepped into an auto-chariot and whizzed by without acknowledging either of them. Her sense of dread had grown and she wanted nothing more than to be gone from this place. Buzzing into place behind it, another chariot, this one forged from pure gold, halted in front of C-ZR and Antony. Brutus was close enough now that he heard C-ZR speaking.

"Let me have men about me that are fat," C-ZR's altered voice box ground out. "Sleek-headed men and such as sleep a-nights. Yond Cassius has a lean and hungry look. He thinks too much. Such men are dangerous." Antony handed a pair of gold-trimmed goggles to C-ZR, who donned them with fluidity of motion suggesting absolute confidence and control. Both qualities Brutus feared.

C-ZR turned his lofty gaze on Brutus. The warmth of Julius shone through the gears and his coal-fired brain. A wisp of a grin spread evenly across his hybridized face. All the days of verbalized combat they engaged in together against the opposition came back to Brutus. He could almost remember his friend's voice before his mechanization. A connection, a thread tying them to each other reached across the mass of people, but Brutus sensed the mechanized implants taking over what was left of his friend.

Antony came forward to C-ZR, slipped a pair of his

own goggles over his eyes, and nodded to the keeper of the auto-chariot. C-ZR's brass eye retracted from Brutus as he mounted the heavily plated transport. He pointed forward. In a matter of seconds, the two of them whisked away out of sight.

With their leader gone, the crowd dispersed quickly back to whatever it was they occupied themselves with before the mandatory gathering in the forum.

When C-ZR bore only the name Julius and hadn't been amalgamated, his every word, every action captivated Brutus. Their friendship remained deep and unmarred for years. But then the mighty man sustained near-death injuries causing the Senate—with him leading the push—to vote for the C-ZR half-casting to commence. Only a vote from the Senate could activate the failsafe to save Julius's life. For hours, his life hung suspended between this one and the next, with the city of the dead yawning wide for this most famous of prey.

"Steam-powr'd thou art with a husk of metal," Brutus said to himself. Cassius kept his head close to his new conspirator as they talked treason, mutiny, death. Brutus touched the tip of the awl-shank again, if only to remind himself of the difficult road he chose. "Once a man with face pure, clean of blemish, thou wast a bright morning star set on us. Upon a time I saw thee set the Gaul to running across the mountains in fear. The giants of the sands of Egypt fled as you wooed the Queen of the Nile for yourself."

Cassius raised his head looking for him. The piston hissed a slow haunting stream of exhaust as it pivoted his arm above his head, signaling Brutus to join them. He could see the winds of change blowing all around them as the crowd broke up and returned to whatever they were doing before C-ZR's arrival. A few words trickling from Cassius' mouth would start a revolt, certainly, but what about Rome?

A vision of first seeing Julius return from his amalgamation into C-ZR filled his mind. Sweeping through the Senate with his newly affixed appendages, eyes, and brain, he swatted a chunk of stone from one of the pillars to demonstrate his newfound might and power.

That day you were re-born was the day you died.

"Now thou has made those who made you high low. Once Julius, now C-ZR first, always with blood of Romans as your pedestal." The awl-shank burned the tips of his fingers as the warmth of his skin brought it life. The handle vibrated as the tip thirsted for a place to burrow itself. "Thou was once my friend, now only C-ZR." Brutus strode toward his compatriots with a renewed vision in his mind, his heart set in stone.

"Now only C-ZR," he said again, this time with his fist clenched tight around the awl-shank. The very tool that would set the world free, and he the only hand that could wield it.

"And if all but C-ZR doth remain, then thy moments of steam are but numbered," he heard himself say. He would never address Julius by that wretched title now or ever again. "Beware the ides of March, indeed."

"Your expanse of metal is a waste of time"
by Frances Hern

Your expanse of metal is a waste of time.
I gave you, Lady Underwood, my trust
That you would whisper words of love sublime,
Savage, extreme, cruel, inciting lust.
Instead you clack and clatter, hiss and jam
Your keys then merely echo what I think.
You give no thought or care to who I am,
The depths to which your failure makes me sink.
I built your slender carriage straight and true,
ran ribbons red and black around your frame,
installed an entire alphabet but you
form words that make no sense. Have you no shame?
Your hulking bulk of rust and mocking bell
have slain my dreams and led me to this hell.

Much Ado About Steam Presses: A Scandal of Minor Importance
by R. J. Booth

John hesitated, and his brother turned.

Benedict, his brother's pompous third-in-command, stopped bickering with the bluestocking niece.

Her cousin, the blushing debutante who had faced John in the receiving lines, from whom he had gleaned such perverse pleasure, as she wavered between the mortal sin of ignoring a guest, and the mortification of *staring* at him; well, she had none of that reluctance about her now.

John looked at the right hand of Leonato Campinelli, and back up. Why had the gruff former official approached him? Surely he realised who John was. The malcontent, the Luddite turncoat; *Il Bastardo*, to the discrete. He who was "not worth the life spared him—*if* one could call it a life..." John harbored no illusion of his standing amongst the Great and Good of New Messina. Pedro had certainly not mentioned him in negotiations; that much he had gathered from the enthusiastic noises and disproportionate back-slapping that had followed.

It was his brother's eyes that John felt most keenly on him now, though he did not look back: The expression never changed. Pedro's face was a wall, and his jaw locked before it. John's knee, quite independent of stimulus, began to itch.

To his left, he noticed Claudio's hand twitched about his hip, where he knew the young lieutenant had always holstered a pocket derringer.

John took the former official's hand in his right and squeezed.

"I thank you," he said, and smiled.

The moment at which Leonato realised his mistake revealed itself only to John, by the merest tremble in the man's facial muscles and a slow reddening of his cheeks. A bead of sweat traced a line from the gentleman's venerated temple towards his fatted neck.

Pedro's face relaxed. Nervous titters decayed once more into vagaries of gossip and other weather; topics more suited to shellacked papier mâché columns, rows of pristine pamphlets on the latest social discourses, or the panharmonium, un-played for at least a fortnight, judging by the dust.

"Please it your grace lead on?" said Leonato.

He took Pedro by the arm, and the two arch-industrialists led the party across the reception hall. John shuffled behind. As he adjusted the deerskin glove over his tempered steel, brass-plated prosthesis, John watched the older man flex his aching hand behind his back.

—∞—

John unfastened the straps that held the apparatus

in place, and set the complex of industrial-grade clockwork next to the unwieldy leg piece on the floor. He arched his shoulders, planted his hand, and with a grunt, hefted his body off the bed.

His shoulder caught on the edge of the window frame, in time to stop his body, but not his thought of smashing through the glass, that long fall. John grinned through perspiration-stuck hair, but as he steadied himself, kept his eye firmly above the horizon.

John followed the steel girders of the tramway as they traced fractals of fleur-de-lis across the bay from New Messina: from the gated mansions and swallowed olive plantations on the hills; through the marbled boulevards, with their copper-capped guildhouses, and smart fountain-blessed walks. Onwards, where the arches shielded the great and good from the horrors of the festering slums and rotting brick shells of the machine-stricken trade district; the shrieking harbour gulls; past the precarious Torre Faro, with the private landing of Leonato Campinelli balanced on its ornamented iron claws; across the Strait and beyond.

For this, John could almost forgive his brother's choice of bolthole. Somewhere beneath this tarnished palimpsest still lay the town he and his brother had once sought to build together; egalitarian and liberated. His chest swelling painfully against the fading serrations of steel across his side, John breathed.

The click of the door knob alerted him to Conrad's presence. The manservant had been particularly swift this time, but John's unwatched moments were rare and he wasn't prepared to acknowledge the start of the charade a moment earlier than he had to.

"What the good-year, my Lord!"

John resigned himself to his fate. His continued insistence on this kind of pathetic sycophancy, seemingly so beloved by his brother these days, irked John considerably. Still, he made no attempt to accommodate Conrad as he fumbled with the leg piece; he saw no reason why he should. John could not remember what first made him suspect the manservant, though he did seem to be of that peculiar breed descended not from apes, but beached jellyfish.

"My Lord," ventured Conrad. "Why are you thus... out of measure sad?"

His clammy hands slipped about the brass plate, and slivers of pain twisted through John's leg. Perhaps what infuriated him most about Conrad was that his brother could have, at least, chosen a man of subtlety to spy on him.

"There is... no measure in the occasion that breeds," said John, wearily, "therefore the sadness is without limit."

"You should hear reason."

For once, John did not have to feign his irritation.

"And when I have heard it, what blessing brings it?"

Conrad developed a sudden interest in the straightness of his white shirt sleeve, a shade that complimented his current complexion most excellently.

"If not a present remedy," he said, at tremulous length, "at least a... patient sufferance."

John looked at the pamphlet that Conrad had clumsily thrust into his hand. The paper, which, conveniently, had just happened to be in the butler's pocket at the time was stamped with the monogram of a well-known Austrian physician; and as John perused it, the pages fell open at a bold-headed chapter, entitled '*THE CASTRATION COMPLEX*'. He smirked; as much at the thought he might have underestimated Conrad's wit, as the more likely faux pas of the supposed gentleman's gentleman.

"I wonder that thou—being, as thou say'st thou art, born under Saturn—" John retorted, "—goest about to apply a moral medicine to a mortifying mischief." John punched a dispenser on the table in the middle of the room, another of Campinelli's conceits, and extracted a cigarillo with theatrical ease.

"'Tis not wisdom," the manservant began, "thus to second grief against yourself..."

"Cease thy counsel," said John. He lit the cigarillo with his Ronson Pist-o-liter and took a draught of smoke, letting it curdle in his lungs.

"I cannot hide what I am," continued John. "I must be sad when I have cause, and smile at no man's jests; eat when I have stomach, and wait for no man's leisure; sleep when *I* am drowsy and tend on no man's 'business'; laugh when I am merry and claw no man in his humour."

"Yea," hissed Conrad, "but you must not make full show of this 'til you may do it without controlment. Your brother hath ta'en you newly into his grace, where it is impossible you should take root but by the fair weather that you make yourself. It is needful that you frame the season for your own harvest."

Even for Conrad, it was a bold gesture; yet John found himself examining the underside of his right arm where the manservant had gripped him. The mechanical prosthesis, procured by Pedro in the wake of his prodigal return, was still unfinished; here the gears were still exposed. Cogs whirred as he clicked his fingers one by one. A thought crossed John's mind, and jarred in his jaw.

"I had rather be a canker in a hedge, than a rose in his grace," John said, but there was no heart in the words. He was twenty miles and months away, at the cliff on which his brother, his half-brother, had finally caught him. With Claudio gone, and his last refuge compromised, there was nothing but the gulls' cries, and the rocks... And the look in his brother's eyes.

"It better fits my blood to be disdained of all, than to fashion a carriage to rob love from any."

What surprised John after all this time was he could still remember every word—the most Pedro had said to him together in years.

"Though I cannot be said to be a flattering honest man, it must not be denied..."

He had said there would be no more running. If in no other promise Pedro had made to him, in this, he had kept his word.

"I am but a 'plain-dealing villain," John laughed to himself. "I am entrusted with a muzzle, and enfranchised," here his hand clanged dully against his leg, "with a clog. If I had my mouth, I would bite. In the meantime, let me be that I am, and seek not to alter me."

"Can you make no use of your discontentment?" said Conrad.

John stubbed out the foul-tasting cigarillo on the table. "I use it only."

The door slammed against the frieze depicting the festival of Bacchanalia, bringing an abrupt end to the noble nose of some inebriated Pan. The vandal stooped for the disembodied piece and stuffed it in the corner of the frame.

"What news, Borachio?"

The scoundrel turned a grin of yellowed teeth between his unshaven cheeks. He was at least loyal. "I come from a great feast," he said, thumbing his lapels. "I can give you intelligence of an intended marriage."

John snorted. "What is he for a fool that betroths himself to unquietness?"

"Marry, it is your brother's right hand."

"Who?" He had not heard those words in a good while. The realisation clapped him like a thunderbolt. "The most exquisite Claudio. A proper squire," John sat down heavily. "Which way looks he?"

"Marry, on Hero, the daughter and heir of Leonato."

"A very forward March-chick," said John. "How came you to this?"

Borachio waited for John to light his cigarillo, to Conrad's displeasure.

"Being entertained for a perfumer, as I was smoking a musty room," he grinned, "comes me 'The Prince' and Claudio, hand in hand in sad conference. I whipped me behind the arras, and there heard it agreed upon that the Prince should woo Hero for himself, and having obtained her, give her to Count Claudio."

John considered the news. "This may prove food to my displeasure. That young upstart hath all the glory of my overthrow. If I can cross him any way, I bless myself every way. You are both sure, and will assist me?"

"To the death, my Lord," said Conrad, a little too enthusiastically.

"Let us to the 'Great Supper'," John said to Borachio, "Their cheer is the greater that I am subdued. Shall we go prove what's to be done?"

"We'll wait upon your lordship," added Conrad.

John firmly closed the door behind them, and hastened to open the window. Claudio may have fooled Pedro thus far, but marriage? Was it necessary, merely to convince his brother of loyalty? John shook his head. Claudio had always wanted to go too far. That extra mile; that was the reason why he was John's first choice of accomplice when he realised where his brother's intentions were leading. Claudio had proved more than up to the task. Amongst the flaming ruins of the Mendici printworks, John had been lifted by a dangerous exhilaration he had not felt since he and Pedro first taken up the cause of the labourers.

John cursed his tardiness. It had been months since Claudio used his falsely won influence to persuade Pedro to bring him back into the family; and for his part, John had duly played the scowling villain of the piece, but he tired of playing games with a drunkard and a fool. If only he could speak to Claudio away from his brother for just a few minutes!

For once, Pedro's fondness for decorum would provide just the right opportunity.

—⁂—

To preserve the mystery of the Masquerade Ball, the formality of presenting the guests had been skipped, yet John and Borachio stepped onto the deck of the *Santa Eustochia* with a laughable measure of anonymity. Despite Pedro's requirement of a cloak, and the remarkable invisibility John's "condition" gave him amongst polite society, there was no mistaking his unarticulated gait; this was without consideration of Borachio's breath and his overwrought shushing.

Borachio, hidden behind a joke-shop clown's mask, wanted to start the business right away, but John held him back. Behind his Pierrot, he was waiting for a fashionable song of the day, one to which all gentlemen would be obliged to ask the ladies to dance, if they valued their delightful company for the rest of the evening.

They did not have to wait long. As Pedro led Hero to a firmly-guarded corner, Claudio sat on the lower deck, watching stoically through his schoolboy visage with one hand on the drinks table. John steered Borachio to the starboard side of the hooded figure in front of them.

"Are you not Signior Benedick?" asked John, as he clapped a hand on the back of Claudio's shoulder; a familiar gesture from their days in hiding. Yet the young man shook, re-fixed his mask, and pulled his cloak around him.

"You know me well," said Claudio, "I am he."

He must be trying to cover himself, John thought.

"*Signor*," he enunciated, in a manner they had often used to mock the conceited soldier. Still Claudio did not correct him. John collected his thoughts and snared an idea.

"Signor, you are very near to my brother in his

love. He is enamoured on Hero; I pray you dissuade him from her, she is no equal for his birth. You may do the part of an honest man in it." John smirked at the childish jape.

There was a pause. "How know you he loves her?"

This was definitely not the way the conversation should be going. "I... heard him swear his affection?" hazarded John.

"So did I too," slurred Borachio, leaning heavily on Claudio's shoulder, "and he swore he would marry her tonight."

Well, that should settle the matter, thought John. If Claudio had not discovered the prank before, he would surely have realised how ridiculous the notion was after that! The man was no fool, after all. Pedro did not make such politically sensitive moves on a whim.

Yet Claudio made no protest at the remark.

"Come," said John, slapping Claudio's shoulder again for good measure, "let us to the banquet."

It was a convenient excuse: In truth, he no longer had the stomach for it. John did not know what disappointed him more: Claudio's reaction to his greeting, or that he had fallen for such a childish trick.

Perhaps Claudio was simply playing him for a fool? John looked back at the cloaked figure through the open doorway. The young man had not moved from the spot, and he thought he could discern Claudio's shoulders shaking.

John told himself he did not care. The one man who stood with him against Pedro's war of industrialisation had betrayed his trust. There was no ruse to lull the *capo della famiglia* into a false sense of security. Claudio truly was Pedro's man. John watched, disgusted, as Borachio slipped to the floor and toasted the prank's success in vomit.

No. He had merely asked Claudio at the wrong time, the wrong place. John ignored Borachio's calls from down the corridor. He would hear from his real partner soon enough.

And so he did: The next morning, in fact. An Invitation to the Nuptials of Hero May Campinelli and Claudio Forabosco, to be held on Campinelli's airship in two days. Produced on Mendici Reprographic Engines, no doubt: There was the telltale smear of ink rollers on the card's reverse. Paying the messenger his due for such strenuous labour, John crumpled the cheap paper in his metallic hand and closed the door.

John unfurled the card with his left, smoothed the creases out, and stood back from the desk. The pathetic ruse had certainly been uncovered; he had never doubted that it would be, of course. Yet there had been no recriminations. The conditions of John's rehabilitation into the family were clear. Pedro would not have hesitated. Then, this presupposed that Pedro had found out.

John picked up the card in his good hand, his first communiqué from Claudio in months. He had checked for any hidden message between the layers of pressed paper, examined it under candlelight for some invisible ink, but found nothing. The thought occurred to him that, should he wish to discuss his intentions, it would be far easier for the young man to contact him than for John to initiate a meeting. There it was confirmed.

John dropped the card onto the desk with a start. Claudio did not intend to meet him. He had not spent these many months cultivating the root of John's revenge, nor a lure to bring him into Pedro's clutches. John cursed. What a damned fool he had been! He had been betrayed. For love.

—⚒—

It was not difficult to arrange a meeting with Borachio away from Conrad. Borachio disliked the fop intensely, while the latter only cultivated his acquaintance for the gathering of intelligence. John could not imagine this being very productive.

"It is so, the Count Claudio will marry the daughter of Leonato." John acknowledged Borachio's arrival by lifting the ball of crumpled paper high above his head. He did not wait for him to respond. "I am sick in displeasure to him, and whatsoever comes athwart his affection rages evenly with mine."

"Yea, my lord, but I can cross it," said the scoundrel.

"Any bar, any cross, any impediment will be medicinable to me. Show me briefly how."

"I think I told your lordship how much I am in the favour of Margaret, the waiting-gentlewoman to Hero."

John shuddered inside. "I remember."

"I can, at any unseasonable instant of the night, appoint her to look out at her lady's chamber window."

The idea spread like fire across John's mind. "What

proof shall I make of that?"

Borachio explained the plot in graphic detail, and with much eagerness, but John was merely nodding along. He had gathered the threads in his mind some moments before. What dominated his thought was the necessity of it all. The woman herself posed no obstacle: If she truly loved Claudio, she would understand. Only a fool would put himself in the hands of his brother; John knew that only too well. He could not abandon Claudio to that fate.

However, there was something of a difference between a mere jape played on a former brother-at-arms, and the disgracing of a lady—and not just any lady, but the daughter of a former government official turned Mafia collaborator. There could be no rehabilitation after that.

John felt a sudden weariness of all this plotting and scheming; the machinations of his brother, the politics of New Messina. He had already fought that battle, in private salons and factory sidestreets, the smell of cheap tobacco and gunpowder blending into one corrupting fume. John spat and Borachio stuttered apologies. It had only made everything worse.

All John wanted now was freedom. He longed to find somewhere where neither his brother's men, nor any of Borachio's ilk could find him. The anarchist was loyal, but cared more for broken machines than the men they put out of work. He could not understand that the issue was of the retention of some form of dignity and continuance; the freedom to be one's own man and what price the true value of this.

Claudio had understood...

"Look you for any other issue?"

John looked at Borachio.

"Only to despite them," he said. "I shall endeavour anything."

—⚡︎—

John hid himself behind a surprisingly tenacious potted *Monstera* until Benedict and Signor Campinelli had passed. It was not the danger of discovery that had almost sent him scuttling from the Mendici airship and back to his room in the tower. John could not understand why he felt so hesitant. He had played the role of the villain for many months now. Yet John kept turning over the plan. It was not too late to stop Borachio, since he not yet paid the man. There would be other opportunities, though likely none so urgent.

Then, he was already knocking at the door, hearing the laughter behind it stop, and a few moments later, standing face-to-face with Pedro.

"My lord and brother," he heard himself say. With some difficulty, John lowered himself on the steel legpiece until he knelt at Pedro's feet. Taking the man's left hand, John closed his eyes—"God save you"—and kissed the cold signet ring.

"Good den, brother," came the reply. The tone was not unkind, but it evinced neither surprise nor fraternal warmth.

With the aid of the doorframe, John braced himself up to standing.

"If your leisure served, I would speak with you," he said.

"In private?"

Behind Pedro, John could see another gentleman straining his neck to see who was at the door. "If it please you; yet Count Claudio may hear, for what I would speak of concerns him." John called over his brother's shoulder. "Means your lordship to be married tomorrow?"

"You know he does."

John swallowed. He could not turn back now.

"I know not that," he said, "when he knows what I know."

To John's astonishment, Pedro then turned his head to Claudio, as if to consult him. Claudio nodded, and the two men helped John through over the threshold to the chair nearest the doorway, which was turned away from the rest of the room. Claudio knelt beside him, while Pedro stood directly in the doorway.

John adjusted the position of his clockwork arm, a gesture of convenient humility. "You may think I love you not," he announced, haltingly. "Let that appear hereafter, and aim better at me by that I now will manifest.

"For my brother," John continued, with one eye on the man, "I think he holds you well, and in dearness of heart hath holp to effect your ensuing marriage—surely suit ill-spent, and labour ill-bestowed."

Aside from refolding his arms, Pedro was as unmoved as Claudio was exasperated.

"If you know of any impediment, I pray you discover it!" Claudio exclaimed.

John briefly spun a few details of the history he had invented together with Borachio, and watched

Claudio's face crumple into tears; as if his heart had broken at the mere suggestion of disloyalty in Hero.

That Claudio so distrusted the love of his life! John was now certain of the nobility of his purpose. Claudio would not suffer long from this mere infatuation. Perhaps John could even persuade Claudio to join him on his escape. It had been a long time since he had a companion truly equal to himself. John smiled to himself, and dismissed a dark thought in the back of his mind.

While Claudio questioned John ever more intently over the details of Hero's supposed infidelity, Pedro listened in silence. Like a statue of a patient Alexander, his face was inscrutable as ever; but behind his eyes John could see the clockwork of Pedro's mind was whirring into new arrangements: To what machinations, he could not gather. John could not hold his brother's gaze.

At last Pedro spoke, only to confirm that, should the accusations prove true, he would provide Claudio with the required moral support. It was all John needed to hear.

The three then departed for the upper deck, from which, as Campinelli seemed unaware, a casual observer might stumble upon a rather indiscreet view onto his daughter's balcony. John led the way, confidence lifting him above his festering doubt.

—⁂—

The wedding of Claudio and Hero was met with a crisp Mediterranean blue from sea to sky: Campinelli's airship had moved to less conspicuous skies for the ceremony. John had more pressing concerns than uninvited daguerrotypists in noisy gyrocopters. Borachio and Conrad were missing, and had been since early morning. The absence of the former could be explained away by the night's labours—or rather, John's payment for them; but that both had failed to return did not bode well.

Neither Pedro nor Claudio mentioned the events of the previous night as they met in the young gentleman's suite. Claudio had regained his composure since then, while Pedro kept his impenetrable mask, now garnished with a reptilian smile. John had his own mask to maintain, though he did not feel the same reticence he had felt before. It was more a detachment, as if the body he inhabited was no longer his, and he was merely watching from a near distance.

The three gentlemen took their positions with the rest of Pedro's immediate entourage at the stern of the great vessel; and to one side of the ruddy-faced Captain. A stringent and constant guardian of the moral fibre of his ship, as he had instructed Claudio earlier; he was smoking fit to match the most industrious of the airship's chimneys.

Of course, John mused privately, it was possible that Pedro planned to expose him at the wedding, leaving him to the mercy of the devastated lovers and their enraged families, as well as the combined private armies of the Campinelli and Mendici families. Something about this struck him as amusing, though it took moments for him to realise he was smiling.

The coughing, card-fed panharmonium announced

the arrival of the bride's party. The engine had been set in motion, and once started, could not be halted.

"Be brief," said Leonato, waving his hand dismissively. "Only to the plain form of marriage,"

The Captain pocketed his Meerschaum and cleared his throat with a deliberate harrumph. "You come hither, my lord," he said, turning to Claudio, "to marry this lady?"

"No."

There were a few titters from the crowd of assembled relatives, and trusted unarmed associates of Campinelli and Mendici.

"To be married *to* her," sighed Leonato, massaging his forehead. "*You* come to marry her."

"Lady, you come hither to be married to this Count?" the officer asked Hero.

Leonato's daughter was a model of bridal virginity: a posy of forget-me-nots and lilies clasped ahead of a bejewelled corset, which seemed to squeeze the spirit from her gut, leaving a lump of pliant motherhood held up in whalebone. In a voice barely audible above the gulls, the young woman affirmed her purpose there.

"If either of you know any inward impediment why you should not be conjoined, I charge you, on your souls, to utter it."

"Know you any, Hero?" Claudio's question was so hard on the heels of the last, it almost snapped at them.

"None, my lord," she answered, honestly.

"Know you any, Count?" asked the Captain.

"I dare make his answer: none," said Leonato.

"O, what men dare do!" Claudio retorted. "What they daily do, not knowing what they do!"

The personal guards of both families came into

sharp focus in the corner of John's eye. He had seen this behaviour from Claudio only once before, in a public house in Aragon. A drunken cove had made insinuations about both the profession and health of Claudio's mother. John recalled with a wry smile how the cure of it had almost cost them their lives.

"Will you with free and unconstrained soul," Claudio said, "give me this maid, your daughter?"

Campinelli had not served the City through the Great Quake of 1908 and its subsequent upheavals for nothing. He could recognise when a young man's temper threatened the peace.

"As freely, son," he replied calmly, "as God did give her me."

"And what have I to give back whose worth may counterpoise this rich and precious gift?" persisted Claudio.

"Nothing, unless you render her again," answered Pedro. And he reached inside the pocket on his steam-jennyed, double-breasted morning suit for a large manila envelope, which he passed to Claudio.

If any member of the wedding party had believed this an act, the illusion was quickly vanishing. Claudio opened the envelope and handed it to a confused Campinelli. Well-respected members of the audience began to heckle the players. The attentions of the armed stewards quelled their enthusiasm.

With one eye on the youth, Campinelli drew out the contents of the envelope, and gave a cry.

"What do you mean, my lord?"

John watched with the interest of a man observing a collision between two steam gurneys; powerless to stop either one, and gripped with a morbid fascination with the inevitable consequence. He knew what was in the envelope: A series of daguerrotypes, printed from the ship's engines last night, and captured at the same hour that John had led Pedro and Claudio to the deck beneath the Campinelli balcony. He had to admit, for all his incompetence, that Borachio played the beast very well.

"Dear my lord," said Campinelli, with the indignation of a man accused of a juvenile transgression long buried in memory, "if you, in your own proof, have made defeat of her virginity—"

"I know what you would say," replied the youth, his cold exterior rapidly melting. "You will say she did embrace me as a husband. No, Leonato. I never tempted her with word too large. Behold how like a maid she blushes here! But she is none. She is more intemperate in her blood than Venus, or those pamper'd animals that rage in savage sensuality!"

Elegant bonnets sank beneath the heads of the crowd. This time, the outcry could not be contained by the guardsmen. A number of gentlemen made protests to representatives of the *Santa Eustochia* on grounds of responsibility for the collective moral fibre: Its chief guardian having excused himself moments earlier.

Leonato stared at the images.

"Are these things spoken or do I but dream?"

"What man was he talk'd with you yesternight out at your window betwixt twelve and one?" Claudio asked of Hero. "Now if you are a maid, answer to this!"

"Seem'd I ever otherwise to you?" stammered Hero.

Claudio turned to the stunned patriarch. "By that

fatherly and kindly power that you have in her, bid her answer truly."

"What kind of catechizing call you this?" exclaimed the lady. "Is my lord well, that he doth speak so wide?"

Leonato replaced the photos back in the manila envelope.

"I charge thee do so…"

"Oh God! How am I beset?"

"I charge thee do so as thou art my child!" demanded Leonato.

"I talk'd with no man at that hour, my lord!" Hero protested through her tears.

"Why, then you are no maiden."

The scene fell silent. In the midst of the pantomime, John had forgotten about his brother. Stunned by the question, the woman made no reply; and Pedro Mendici heaved a sigh heavy with the pathos of a gentleman wronged by someone in whom he had placed great faith. Something turned behind John's mask of calm and began to squirm.

"Leonato," Pedro continued, "upon mine honour, myself, my brother, and this grieved Count did see her, hear her at that hour last night talk with a ruffian at her chamber-window"—Pedro shook his head, and the thing in John's mind twisted—"who hath indeed, most like a liberal villain, confess'd the vile encounters they have had a thousand times in secret."

The thing itched and burned black, as if caught in the embers of some devilish fire.

"I am sorry you must hear. *I* stand dishonour'd that have gone about to link my friend to a common—"

"Fie!"

The burning thing erupted in full conflagration, burning and consuming, pulling John back to his body. He could see only red fumes.

"Fie," John seethed. "They are not to be nam'd, my lord. Not to be spoke of! There is not chastity enough in language without offence to utter them. She's but the sign and semblance of her honour. Out on thee! Seeming! Is this the Prince? Is this the Prince's brother? Is this face Hero's? Are our eyes our own? What authority and show of truth can cunning sin cover itself withal! Thus, pretty lady, I am sorry fo–"

His eyes caught hers in mid-speech, and the molten flow of words stopped. Crumpled in white lace, cotton and silk, Hero lay pale, like a broken porcelain doll, at the feet of Claudio.

A veil of memory, of rocks and spray, drew briefly across John's inner vision, and his heart itched against the thing on his chest. There seemed to be barely enough left of her to pity.

"I am sorry," he finished, haltingly, "for thy much misgovernment."

—⚡—

As Pedro's entourage strode through the ship, John took his place by his brother's side. Since his return to the fold, John had not felt it was proper for him to be there. Now it did, and for all the wrong reasons.

As they turned down the corridor to the Mendici quarters, Pedro glanced over his shoulder at John, and for the merest fraction of a second, John thought he saw him grin.

In that moment, in the finest clarity, a number of things began to make sense: His isolation from Claudio. His brother's choice of sanctuary. Claudio's decision to take his pocket derringer the day they arrived.

John felt a curious sensation coming over him. It was a feeling that, at first, he had some difficulty in ascribing to a particular source, but it spread so persistently and so strongly, that he had to succumb to it. It was as if all the things around him, all these gaudy trappings of a life that placed no value on the work of others, began to take on an unreal quality, and in turn spread that essence to all they touched.

To Don Pedro, and all he had come to represent for John—his brother's attempt to murder him, and his virtual incarceration in his prosthetics. To Claudio, his supporter and his betrayer, and to his anguish and heartbreak. To the pain of Hero, the fury of Leonato and out across the myriad intricate webs that bound the families of New Messina. If any of them suffered, John felt it not with the righteousness of an avenging angel, or even the relief of a songbird freed from a gilt cage.

Later, as John removed the leg prosthesis with its tiny tracking device and discarded it in the air cruiser docking bay, he knew it would not be long before his brother found him. The customary justice would be meted out. Whether this had been worth what brief freedom it earned him, mattered not. His position in the long game had been fixed long ago, and what had necessitated his placing in this strange series of events was beyond his concern. Finally, he understood.

Thoughts of Borachio briefly came to his mind, and John found he was struggling to stifle a laugh. After all, he was merely a plain-dealing villain.

"My brasswork's gleam is nothing like the sun"
by Alia Gee

My brasswork's gleam is nothing like the sun;
Jules Verne is far more read than my notebooks read;
If steam is white, why then my work is done;
If veins be pipes, black pipes flow through my shed.
I have seen science "de-bunked," left and right,
But no such shame see I in my cheeks;
And in some music is there more delight
Than in the noise that from my foes now squeaks.
I love to hear steam shriek, yet well I know
That peacocks have a far more pleasing sound.
I grant I never saw an airship go;
My fire, when it spreads, will burn the ground.
And yet, by heaven I think my lab as rare
As any shop that made the neighbors stare.

Leo's Mechanical Queen
by Claudia Alexander

Part 1 – Port au Prince [1891]

"She is spread of late into a goodly bulk!"

Antigonus grinned to himself, betraying nothing on his face. The damning words came from among the assembly of the fine, and high, of Port au Prince, in a voice loud enough to be heard over the orchestra, and when they died away, the whole assembly rose to their feet, turning to see the Queen.

Hermione drifted in, late again! A very fair-skinned young lady–Creole, mind you, Antigonus thought, with long black hair, smoothed now with the hot comb. The train of her cuirasse dragged along the marble floor, a jewel-encrusted, clock-like pendant from around her neck sparkled in the fashionable, new electric lights.

Most of the men in the room admired her surreptitiously. And *Hougan* Antigonus watched them all from a place beside the king's dais.

In the ballroom, crowded with Haiti's leading families, women in long ruffled dresses with hoops had been doing the 'shuffle'–skirts held out wide with both hands, making sweeping motions with skirts and feet—motions that revealed lacy ankle boots underneath.

Leo, known as 'Monsieur,' king of Haiti, cacique of its people, sat on his cacique's chair on the dais, his cacique's pallium thrown back, under a life-sized portrait of Agassou—the Haitian Loa and guardian of Yoruba traditions. Traditional *trouvé* fires lined the room. More than decorative, they created steam, and were part of an ancient African heritage of engineering and surveying.

Like his ancestors, Antigonus was used to finding a path between extremes, though he didn't do it with surveying instruments. As a priest of Voudon traditions and a Hougon, Antigonus wore his appearance like a mask: tooth missing, scruffy top hat, *ileke* necklaces—indicating proficiency within his religious order—loud colors, face painted with a star around one eye, drawing purposeful contrast to the appearance of the others. Nobody really 'saw' Antigonus under the scruffy hats and dog-eaten boots he wore to every occasion. Only his wife, and she was blind.

If engineers tried to find the minimum point, he tried to find that path of least resistance. So he could appreciate Leo.

Even though Leo's complexion was black as the wings of a magpie, as cacique, Leo was the tribal chieftain of all peoples of mixed African, French, and Arawak-Tiano Indian heritage on the island of Hispaniola. His features were those of his Tiano ancestors—high cheekbones, narrow nose, even lips. Even as a boy, they say, when he visited places like New Orleans or Atlanta, he was accorded the recognition attributed to an indigenous chieftain—like some sort of Seminole or

Chocktau. He embodied different traditions. And he carried himself like a king.

Yet, though master of this island, Leo's only significant role was to assure the *Trouvé* fires kept going. That must rankle an egotist like Leo, Antigonus thought. The dichotomy between the mountain of status and the nadir of his function was the source of the perpetual tension between the Bokor of the island, and the cacique.

"Have you not seen, Antigonus?" Leo grabbed a glass from his butler and downed it in one gulp. "My wife's a hobby-horse, and deserves a name as rank as any flax-wench that puts out."

"Our gracious Queen?" Antigonus shifted from foot to foot. *That don't sound right.* Though everybody knew her to be a protégé of the Governor-General of slave-holding Louisiana, and who was known to have remained on friendly terms with the Governor-General despite her recent marriage to Monsieur.

In the post-Napoleonic world, Haiti was the premiere kingdom for peoples of African heritage in the world, being a free republic. That bastard, Napoleon, re-enslaved the territories under French control outside of France—the overseas so-called *Départements* or *Communitiés*. But Haiti liberated itself of France in the huge African uprising led by Toussaint L'Ouveture.

The French *Départment* formerly known as Louisiana encompassed a sizable piece of the continent of North America, equal in size to the slave-holding United States. The Governor-General was a frequent visitor to Haiti, having been a boyhood friend of Leo's, and had introduced him to his wife, the lovely Hermione.

"Inch-thick, knee-deep," Leo hissed. "Cuckold-isation, my friend. Many a man finds his pond fished by his next door neighbor, by Sir Smile. The planet is mo' bawdy. East, west, north, and south, many thousands have the disease, and are stupidly unaware."

Leo continued loudly, staring at Hermione, voice cracking, almost choking with bile. "There is a plot against my life, my crown."

Out of the corner of his eye, Antigonus could see the Queen and the others staring, open-mouthed. In a timely bit, the orchestra chose that moment to conclude its piece and switch to another. Dead silence permeated the room.

"What!" Hermione colored visibly, large dots of amber shading her complexion, and she stammered. "Monsieur, you mistake."

As the faint strains of a syncopated version of the massive hit *After the Ball* came again from the ballroom floor: "I believed her faithless..." Leo pointed directly at Hermione. "The Governor-General has made you swell thus."

"What is this?" said Hermione at last, "sport?"

Hermione's face exhibited a curious confluence of emotion, an aspect like that of a carnival doll frozen in time forever in a surprised, nonplussed, lassitude—as if a dog had taught a monkey to bark.

"No mistake." Leo slammed his *babalawos* staff against the floor. "Away with her! To prison!"

The guards, startled, hesitated long enough for the company to surge around the Queen.

Hermione spoke again. "What I am to say but that which contradicts my accusation?" she said. "It shall scarce boot me to say 'not guilty,' mine integrity being counted falsehood."

Antigonus snatched his hat from off his head and moved to stand before the Queen himself. "Be certain what you do, Monsieur." He used that deep rich voice to command the attention of the entire assembly. "Your justice may prove a boomerang," said Antigonus, "in which three suffer, yourself, your queen, and the child."

Leo waved a hand. "Shall I be heard?"

Another of their family friends rose to his feet, "Monsieur, be cured of this diseased opinion. I dare my life to say that the Queen is spotless in the eyes of heaven."

Leo stood. "Shall I be heard?" he asked again.

The guards finally positioned themselves around the Queen, and prepared to take her by the arms.

Hermione took out the clockwork brass symbol from around her neck and stared at it in shock. "Some ill planet reigns: I must be patient till the heavens look with an aspect more favorable. Good my lords," she addressed herself to the other gentry present, "I am not prone to weeping, but I have that honorable grief lodged here which burns worse than tears!" She looked around for her attendants, hand on her abdomen. "My women must be with me. For you see my condition." Then she addressed Leo once more. "Adieu, Monsieur. I never wished to see you grieved, nor unhappy, nor troubled of mind."

—⚭—

"Here she come," Antigonus spoke softly to himself.

His wife came, just like they agreed. Leo didn't see her yet.

A young-old looking woman approached the audience room in a shuffling, mincing motion, a bundle in her arms. The sentries shrank from her.

The captain of the day inched forward. "Mambo Paulina?"

In an authoritative voice–one used to giving orders and being obeyed–the young-old looking woman spoke. "Conduct me to the cacique."

"I may not, madam, I have express commandment." The *capitaine* twisted his baton in his hands.

Out of nerves, Antigonus thought as he watched the *capitaine* with his baton from the audience chamber, not out of an intention to use it on Paulina.

"Don't make me choose between you and Monsieur, please, Mambo," the *capitaine* continued miserably.

Ignoring him, Mambo Paulina shuffled past the guards directly into the audience chamber.

"The good Queen has had a girl-child," Paulina announced. The baby in her arms smelled of lavender and orange peel, creating a presence in the enormous chamber, small as she was.

Leo whirled on him. "Antigonus, I charged you that she should not come about me. Now she brings a baby."

"I told her. But you know how womens are." Affection crowded his voice. His wife would make mince-meat out of most men.

"What? Can't rule her?"

"When she take the reins, I let her run."

Coming alongside, Paulina addressed Leo. "What torments, tyrant, have you for me? Wheels? Racks?

Fires? Thy tyranny together working with thy jealousies!"

Antigonus attempted to intercede, but Paulina pushed him aside.

"What flaying? Boiling? In leads or oils? What old or newer torture must I receive? Whose every word deserves to receive of thy worst."

"She not just 'Mambo,' she is 'Bokor,'" Antigonus explained patiently, while still trying to hold Paulina back, "descended from the most powerful of priests. Mambo Paulina's ancestor conducted the most important Voudon ceremony in history. The one that saw us liberated from the French." And once again they'd arrived at one of those sources of conflict between the cacique and the island's religious orders.

"Next was the *Napoleon Intervention.* Napoleon refused Jefferson's offer for Louisiana, all right. The Voudon drums rang out all night," Antigonus clapped his hands, "and Napoleon didn't sell!" He allowed his own laughter to ring out and echo from the walls.

Leo wasn't paying him no mind, staring as he was at Paulina. A dangerous path, this. Cliffs on either side. It would not do to make this a conflict between Bokor and cacique.

"*Bon Dieu!* A nest of traitors," hissed Leo.

"I am none." Antigonus snatched his hat off and bowed his head.

Paulina did not follow suit, and held her silence.

"*Delala.* Gross hag," Leo cried, voice dripping with sarcasm, using the Creole slang term for a crazy person. "I'll have you burnt."

"Fancies too weak for boys, too green and idle for

girls of nine—think what they have done! Cruel usage of your Queen savors of tyranny. I'm not the crazy person here!" Paulina threw her head back and stared at Leo with what they both knew were disorienting eyes, devoid of pupils.

"Out!" Leo hissed. "I'll not rear another's issue."

Paulina shrugged off the security detail and turned away with her shuffling gait. "Do not push me, I'll be gone soon enough. Look to your babe, Monsieur. 'Tis yours."

Antigonus moved in between his wife and the cacique and then saw a cunning look pass across the face of the cacique.

"What will you venture to save this bastard's life?" Leo settled back down in his chair.

"Anything, Monsieur, that is within my ability." He would do anything to prevent a schism between the Bokor and the cacique.

"Swear that you will perform my bidding." Leo held out the *Osun*, the emblem at the top of his *babalawos* staff that was the symbol of his authority.

Antigonus reached out his hand to touch the *Osun*, a twisting feeling in his gut telling him a trap was coming.

"We enjoin you to carry this female bastard to some remote place out of our dominions, and there leave it."

"Umph, umph umph." Antigonus pursed his lips and spoke those three West African beats, punctuations that could be used to mean almost anything. Eshu must be laughing at him now.

"All rise."

The world masked to her, Paulina could distinguish very little, just differences of light and dark. From the rustling chairs, Paulina presumed Leo and his advisors had situated themselves in the courtroom.

"This session, to our great grief, tries our wife, much beloved by all."

"Umm-hmm." Affirmations rang out in the audience.

"Let us be cleared of being tyrannous. Since we so openly proceed in justice. Which shall have its due course, even to the guilt or the purgation. Produce the prisoner."

Paulina heard the sweep of silk against the floor, the warm temerity of the Queen's presence, an emotional beacon as she was ushered into the room. Papers shuffled at the podium, and with a deep intake of breath the officer of the court began to speak.

"Hermione, Queen to His Excellency, Leontes, President-for-life, and cacique of Haiti."

While the reading continued, Paulina floated on memory. There was her grandfather, stirring sausage into a big pot of gumbo. *I'm befuddled, Baba.* In her little girl's voice she used the affectionate term 'Baba' for a prominent male figure. *Something is wrong.*

"... Here accused and arraigned of high treason, in committing adultery with the Governor-General of Louisiana..."

The audience gasped with every word that received special emphasis by the officer of the court.

"... And conspiring to take away the life of our sovereign cacique. The pretense whereof being thou, Hermione, didst counsel and aid them, to fly away by night, contrary to the faith and allegiance of a subject."

The audience gasped. These were not gasps of horror but of baser emotions, and Paulina winced at the anticipation in the room.

"*There'll come a time, girl,*" her grandfather, the *Bokor*, Hezekiah, part of the sect responsible for the Napoleon Intervention, handed her a spoon, "*when all the prayers, and herbs, and drums, and* gris gris, *won't be enough, when all your magic will seem to dry up like a teapot that's been left too long.*"

"Umph," Paulina muttered, and then realized Hermione had been speaking for quite some time.

"... at Werlein Hall, at the ball of the Twelfth Night Revelers. You were *Le Roi de la Feve*, and I found the golden *feve*... and became your queen for the evening."

Paulina heard the tears in Hermione's voice. And, though she was sure Leo would never release them, from the warmth in his face, tears welled in Leo's eyes. Paulina nodded, but her neck and shoulders were stiff with tension, like a coil of wire in a brass spring.

"For the Governor-General, I do confess an affection as one has for a kindly elder brother. But now, like Anne Boleyn, I find myself on every street-corner proclaimed a strumpet."

The audience, whether punctuating this speech with cries of 'Amen,' 'Ago,' or simply 'Umph,' brought a swift, retaliatory, pounding from the podium.

"You had a bastard by the Governor-General. And as you are past all shame—so thou shalt feel our justice."

Paulina felt the tension ratchet up inside her body, even as Leo, with the constant sounds of pounding of his *babalawos* staff, to someone trained in the path of *Ifa*, raised the level of disquiet in the room.

"As thy brat hath been cast out, so do I pronounce upon thee: death."

The audience performed a collective intake of breath. And just there, just as Leo pronounced the word, Paulina felt it. Like a moth's wing against the canopy of her mind, a gleeful coo, a child feasting on a gum drop. She stretched her head far back, straining to 'see,' while Hermione continued to speak.

"Spare your threats, Monsieur. The bug with which you would fright me, I seek."

"–Umm-hmm." The audience seemed to be greatly entertained by Hermione's prideful response.

"To me can life be no commodity: The crown and comfort of my life, your favor, I do feel it gone, though I know not how it went. My second joy and first-fruits of my body, from her presence I am barred, like one infectious. Lastly, hurried here to this place..."

Amidst the bedlam of agitated emotion in the arena, Paulina could 'see' even less that before. The unquiet as good as cast a blanket of darkness over the room, blinding her, in truth. Jealousy, thought Paulina a warding hand on her *ikele* necklace. Wielded by one of the Bokor of Haiti's ancient enemies. If she was right, this Loa would swallow all in its path.

"Monsieur, tell me what blessings have I, that I should now fear to die?" came Hermione's strong voice. "If I shall be condemned upon surmises, all proofs only what your jealousies awake, I tell you 'Tis vanity and not law."

"That's right," said some in the audience.

She stretched to distract the spirit. *As the case now*

stands, it is only a curse. He cannot be compell'd to't. But even as the pushed into the mental world, marching footsteps distracted her.

"Stop!" Paulina commanded. But her voice was consumed in commotion, 'unquiet,' and ghoulish mental laughter.

Around the enclosure, from all sides, came whirling, whirring sounds—a blade moving through the air. Squinch, came a horrifying sound. Followed by a thud that was drowned in a tremendous rumbling from the assembly. *Non!* Paulina felt the taste of okra—her grandfather's lesson on failure—and knew she had four minutes.

Paulina, hand on her *ikele* necklace, went to work. *Noir,* she commanded. Trade clarity for herself with darkness for the rest, emotionally and physically. As soon as she did, she saw as if in a photographic negative, Hermione's head on the floor, mouth screaming but making no sounds other than bloody splutters. *Bonne fortune. Still conscious.* She absorbed the visceral emotions of the dying queen: the horror of knowing she'd been separated from her body, an agonizing concern about how difficult this was going to be for her daughter. *Thank the Loa. Emotion. Something to work with.*

She must use the *kosi idina*, an incantation to remove physical obstacles and spatially translate three bodies— herself, Hermione's head, rapidly losing blood, and Hermione's body still twitching uncontrollably with traumatic nerve damage.

"The heavens themselves do strike at my injustice." Leo's voice rose over the sound of thunder and barrage of unnatural lightning that even Paulina could sense. "Loa, pardon my great profaneness. For being transported by my jealousies to bloody thoughts."

Then he called for her, "Mambo!"

But Paulina had no time for him now.

—⁂—

Mambo never called for him to visit. When Leo stepped over the threshold of her sanctuary, many months later, dressed in frock coat, top hat, vest, it was with sweaty palms.

And just as he expected, she was going to make him wait.

A huge elevated fire pit, the *Trouvé* fire—always burning for as long as Leo had known Mambo—occupied one corner. *Trouvé* fires helped power the special technology in which the priests of the island specialized. Fire created both steam and a vacuum, and the uses of fire for vacuum originated back with Heron of Alexandria, in Egypt thousands of years before.

Mambo liked to have a trumpet player around and a group of drummers. There they were now, slapping their thighs in a 2/3 rhythm accompanied by cries of *aloo-aah*. Normally, music made Leo feel alive, but today he felt like his tongue was permanently stuck to the roof of his mouth.

Occupying another large corner of the room was mo' newer construction. He smelled the pine scent of sawdust but the whole thing was hidden behind a canvas. It looked like that portion of the room had been sectioned off to create a sort of shrine.

The table was set for quite a few guests but Leo

knew, with a chill, that the Mambo expected only his company this afternoon. Other settings were in place to honor the ancestors–should any of them intend to call. *Dementia.* He recognized the death card among the tarots that were scattered across the table in a lazy profusion. Very ominous, he thought. *As if the practitioner can't move on.*

The most arresting part of the room sported an assortment of huge masks. Each one starkly white, in contrast to the orange dust of the floor. Leo gasped. *Masks of Hermione!* He edged closer.

From the white forehead of one burst enormous horns of red and ochre. *That's mo' difficult to comprehend and not a little demented.* From the eyes of the next one, block-like resistors and capacitor-things stuck out, like the tube eyes mounted on a crayfish. *Unnatural.* One resembled a female face, but with grotesque red lips, and viper hair made of wire, which wriggled in a wild snake-like profusion.

Leo shook his head. The Bokor held odd ideas about death, that much he knew. White represented the color of death–as a veritable inverse of the person in life, presenting their spirit. Beyond that, he was unable to comprehend what these horrific visions were intended to convey.

Mambo Paulina entered the room at last with her shuffling walk. Leo remembered the last painful conversation they had where he'd called her a hag. Evidently the Mambo did too, because her face crinkled into a grimace.

"Monstrous, the casting forth of your baby-daughter." Paulina put a large kettle into the hearth, and set out a couple of tea cups. "Then you made my husband, Antigonus, choose: devotion to country and duty, or to all things natural. Though a devil would have shed water out of fire ere done't."

Leo shuddered when those eyes with no pupils fixed on him.

"The wide Saragossa Sea. Know what happens to sailors who enter that forbidden place?"

Her sightless eyes, now seemingly focused out the window could see his every feature. That Leo knew.

"Gulf weed."

A picture of the plant she was referring to sprang into Leo's mind. Tough, pale brown sea-weed. Multitude of small air-bladders to keep it aloft. Infested with barnacles, crabs, sea lice. Formed a sort of carpet on top of the water. Leo wrinkled his lips in distaste.

The Saragossa was famous as a ghastly resting place for mariners. A skiff becalmed there accumulated the weed around its hull. If the ship was unable to clear the weed, the crew died slowly of thirst and starvation. The vessel would poke around, manned only by the ghostly remains until, sails rotten, rigging frayed, hull eaten by teredo worms, the whole thing sank.

Was that the fate of Antigonus? Leo heard his own breath, as he inhaled deeply into his lungs. Mambo's expression of face was so hard to read with her eyes the way they were. Leo found himself wriggling like a schoolboy.

Paulina poured water over a red powdery substance and handed him the tea. When he shrank from it, she cackled.

"Afraid to take a glass from old Paulina? Afraid of

the potion that it might contain?"

I am the cacique, she wouldn't dare.

"Maybe it contains a bath for the soul?"

Paulina opened the aromatic pouch and allowed him to inspect the reddish leaves, ochre peppercorns, and beige pumpkin seeds. "But the last," Paulina set the kettle onto the furnace again. "Oh lords, the Queen, the Queen."

"Think of me!" Leo exclaimed. "I'm the one now heirless, having destroyed the sweetest companion that ever man hoped of."

Leo still sometimes felt as if his head were going to explode like it did the day of that unnatural trial, with a tightness in his chest that made him feel as if he were being driven, like a racing steed to the finish line.

"Well, as to that. I have a gift for you. But before I pull the drawstring, I have a question."

Oh, God. Leo rubbed his hand over his abdomen, to no avail.

"About your wedding festival," said Paulina fumbled around the living quarters, holding on to the furniture, feeling her way toward the new construction.

Was she worse blinder than before? Leo took a draught of tea, checking again for weird smells. Cinnamon. Pepper. You never knew.

"Came there a knock at the door in the dead of the night? When all were gone but yourselves."

"*Non.*" Leo put down the cup, only too relieved to dive into a happy memory. "We were too..." She'd abandoned her corset, and hadn't been wearing anything but a pair of silk knickers. "Wait now." There was something. "Now you mention it, yes. We were quite alone." Leo leaned forward. "I got up to see, and Hermione nearly tackled me trying to get me not to open the door."

Leo recovered from memory to find Paulina staring out of the window, sightless eyes wide. "And?"

"I opened the door." Leo waved a hand in the air. "Nobody. Nothing."

"Umph umph umph," Paulina said with those three expressive West African beats.

Leo was stumped. He had no idea what Paulina's expressions signified. "Nothing there, I'm telling you."

"Maybe it was an *Abiku*, come a'callin' to see what mischief she could do."

What's an Abiku? Leo wanted to ask, but Mambo seemed busy.

"Jealousy is a precious creature," she whispered as if conversing with one of the ancestors for whom the table was set, "calling forth extraordinary passions. As she's rare, must it be great, and as his person's mighty, must it be violent, and as he does conceive he is dishonored by a friend which ever professed to him, why, his revenge must be the more bitter."

Paulina turned away from her private conversation, moved to draw aside the curtain, and Leo's palms began to sweat again.

Under the canvas was a chamber of the most perfectly symmetrical glass Leo had ever seen. *Magically constructed.* And inside, on a pedestal, well, he was no sculptor but even he could tell it was an incredibly well-drawn likeness of Hermione, her proportions, her posture and bearing. Yet, her formerly luminous honey-colored skin was now grey with a purple tinge.

A sloppy wig had been unceremoniously slapped onto her bald head, and a veil covered her face.

"I like your silence. It shows off your wonder."

Leo stood and circled the shrine to study Hermione from all angles. Had they stuffed her body, taxidermy style? He could see where they'd stuck her head back on her neck with pretty sophisticated wiring, but other than that he could see no discernable... He tried the glass door. "Can I go in?"

The outer door sprang open at his touch with a soft 'whoosh' as smooth and easy as the sound of the horn players outside. Leo leapt back, then tightened his lips. Almost none of Mambo's magic frightened him. Almost. But the Bokors of Haiti were famous for their morbid creations... what the Americans and English called 'zombies.'

"*Non!*"

Mambo's voice was just a little too strident. Leo was not fooled. "A *revenant?*" Leo whirled on Paulina. "Please no, Mambo."

"And if you could choose between having her back, and a *revenant?* Which would it be?"

Leo couldn't keep the disappointment out of his voice. He tried to imagine soulless eyes turned on him, waiting his command—without laughter, without understanding. "Please, Mambo." He brought sweaty palms together in supplication. Wild thoughts careened in his brain.

Did the Mambo intend for him to be strangled in the night by his queen's zombie? Come to life to visit revenge upon her murderer? He wondered fleetingly if Mambo had a way of making the statue animate, and glanced again, in vain, for signs of life. How tempting to believe that the rambunctious Hermione could be returned, that death could be a gateway to life. But only a simpleton would crave such a rejuvenant.

"I never asked for something like this."

"*Imbecile.*" Paulina leaned toward him, face stretched into a broad crocodile grin. "My husband, Antigonus. You made him choose," she whispered, "between you and me!..."

"A *revenant* has no soul, Mambo."

Paulina nodded toward the statue and raised her eyebrows. "... Your turn. Do you trust me?"

"No, please, Mambo." She had to be brought to see the truth of this, he reasoned.

She took his hand in her icy cold fingers, her grip as strong as any of his rivals from his youthful boxing days.

Leo struggled to unclasp his fist. "It's my fault because I opened the door?"

"You opened the door." Paulina agreed.

Her face contained a certain fury. He tasted a coppery flavor in his mouth. *A man doesn't allow himself to be ruled by a woman.* The words almost burst out of his mouth with all the vehemence that he could muster.

"You're showing your club foot," Paulina said through clenched teeth, as if she knew every thought in his head.

"You strike me sorely to say I did it..."

"A man," she put emphasis on the word, "has to examine himself."

"I confess and lament the manner of the queen's death, how she came to't bravely," Leo struggled against being forced to his knees.

"The dignity of this act was worth the audience of kings and princes." Paulina seemed to commend him for this admission, the force of her grip continuing to give efficacy to her accusations. "And yet there was more than one person harmed by your profaneness, and who has a right for their life to be re-engineered."

"Your pity does my deeds make the blacker." Leo gasped. "Let us hence, where we may leisurely each one demand an answer to his part."

"For ever unvenerable be thy hands if you cannot be quit of thy great indiscretion."

Leo looked down at his hands, fast being crushed, and contrary words died on his lips. "Thou canst not speak too much. I deserve all the bitter talk. Thou didst speak but well and mostly the truth; which I receive much better than to be pitied of thee." He stood and looked again at Hermione. "Prithee, allow me to here visit the dead body of my queen. Upon this sanctuary shall the cause of her death appear, unto my shame perpetual. Once a day I'll visit this chapel where she rests, and tears shed here shall be my recreation. So long as nature will bear up with this exercise, so long I daily vow to use it. Come and lead me unto these sorrows."

Part 2 – New Orleans, Seventeen years later.

"Napoleon didn't sell," Deuberry gave the familiar salutation at the back door.

The doorman grinned, and held the curtain aside for him. "She in here."

"An old man is working in the field, when who should appear beside him but the Devil himself!" A comedian, a white man in blackface, practiced his lines on the stage. "'Do you like eggs?' asks the Devil just as calm as you please. This old Niggah isn't phased one bit. 'Yep,' he says without even looking up. And the Devil up and disappears, just as fast as he appeared." The comedian, spoke from the stage to a largely empty theater, as the staff of the Baronne de Carondelet worked readying the venue for the evening's performance.

"Seventeen years later, the Devil come along again. And this old Niggah, he still out there, working those fields. Devil say, 'How?' Old Niggah say 'Fried!'"

Deuberry loved that old joke. There, but by the grace of God, went him. Formerly a man of Leo's household in Haiti, Deuberry had worked for the Governor-General of Louisiana these seventeen years, helping Mambo Paulina fix the damage done by Leo's jealousy.

Silent, the theater staff went about their tasks. A slender young woman, a *madias* rag on her head, cleaned the stage with mop and pail, on hands and knees. Those high cheekbones, and Indian features. At last Deuberry pulled out an old wrinkled sepia letter from Mambo Paulina with the cryptic message: *Find the heir of Leontes.*

So Antigonus had brought her here. To New Orleans. All those years they'd been looking for a light-skinned baby—a girl-child who bore a resemblance to Hermione, or worse, to the Governor-General. So they'd searched all the *Sociétés des Amis des Noirs.* They'd gone over to Fisk University to look for adoptions among the Creole. It was only recently that rumors surfaced of an obvious bastard of Leontes, doing hard labor on one of the sugar plantations. After nightfall, she came into town—for more work.

Deuberry stiffened watching a brown-skinned fellow chatting with her while she did her chores, hanging off the piano bench. "Who's this now?"

This dude, having decked himself out in the bola feathers of one of the acts, punched the keys and sang with a raw intensity, though he had no skill whatsoever on the piano. "*Yo* mama don't wear no *Draws; Ah* seen her when she took 'em *Off—*"

The young woman didn't speak, but when she turned to look at the young man at the piano, bringing her face momentarily into the light, the cant of her head and the disapproving-nonetheless-amused-but-mostly-think-of-the-consequences carriage of her mouth conveyed as eloquently as words: 'Get down from there.'

Through her cotton chemise, Deuberry saw shapely shoulders and upper arms. Figures she wasn't upstairs with the whores. A hard body was no delight for gentlemen who came to the club.

"She soaked 'em in alco*Hol*; She sold 'em to Santy *Claus*," sang the young man, broad grin on his face, eyes never leaving the young woman.

Deuberry put an arm up against the theater curtains and watched, and after a few minutes found his face too long stretched into a laugh.

"He told her 'twas 'gainst the *Law*; To wear them dirty *Draws*."

"Perdita!"

The young woman jerked at the sound. One of the whores upstairs was calling her, Deuberry surmised.

"Nigger, get up here."

The doorman strolled into the auditorium and climbed the stairs to chase the young man away. "Niggah, you's wasting time here. Be gone with you."

"Beggin' your pardon, sir," the big man returned the feathers before scooting off the piano bench.

"What's your name?" asked Deuberry when the young man was before him.

"Autolycus is my name, but folks just call me 'Cus."

"What sort of name is that?"

"They's always cussin' at me."

'Cus opened a leather knapsack for Deuberry to inspect, full of secondhand trinkets and home-made baubles, including several bottles labeled 'Nature's True Remedy.' "Ain't a counterfeit among them." He pointed to each in turn, "not a ribbon, pomander, brooch, table-book, knife, tape, glove, shoe-tie, bracelet, or horn-ring."

"You're a businessman, then?"

'Cus looked stunned. Then a slow grin spread over

his face. "Who dat say I'm a businessman! You looking for Perdita? She his daughter then? He looking for her now?"

"Perdita's her name?" Deuberry wondered if Antigonus had named her thus. It meant 'lost.' "The Governor-General wants to see her. Tonight."

When 'Cus straightened, eyes widened, Deuberry took him by the arm. "A cause more promising," Deuberry nodded to 'Cus's feathers and knapsack, "a dedication of yourselves to unpathed waters, undreamed shores."

'Cus raised one hand to his mouth. "Ain't that some shit!"

She possessed Hermione's walk, Deuberry surmised watching Perdita and her friend careen down the hallways of the newly refurbished Denechaud Hotel like two drunken sailors, gawking at everything.

"We're a couple of swells, we stay at the best hotels," 'Cus mimicked the voices of white vacationers while he examined the electric lights, then ran to catch up with Perdita, who was marching along.

Deuberry motioned them toward the iron gates of the spanking new lift. "We'll take the elevator." The New Hotel Denechaud proclaimed itself the first ever to install one in New Orleans, and the white Governor-General chose the forward-looking establishment as a venue in which to conduct his unofficial business.

Both of them gaped at him.

"Shit," said Perdita.

"Shhh..." 'Cus tried to cover her mouth with his hand. "Girl, you better get 'customed to more genteel speaking, 'cause genteel ways is going to be life or death for you now."

Perdita turned to Deuberry, eyes on the floor. "Your pardon, sir."

Deuberry ushered them inside, greeted the doorman, who likewise gawked to see blacks not in the service entrance.

"You works the elevator like this." The doorman slid the grating closed, cranked the handlebar in place, and depressed a large black button to engage the motor.

Perdita yelped when the elevator began its ascent. "Shi–"

"Shhhh," said 'Cus.

"Niggah, please!"

"The Vanderbilts have asked us up for–tea." 'Cus, thumbs in his suspenders, stuck a pinky finger out and wagged it. "But we don't know how to get there, no sirree."

Deuberry escorted them to an expansive suite with brocade curtains, gilded portraits on the wall, from which they could see down Poydras Street. 'Cus fell silent.

Deuberry climbed the stairs to the sleeping quarters to confer with the Governor-General and prepare him for this interview, but he found the Governor-General watching already from a crack in the door, pipe in hand.

Deuberry couldn't remember when he'd smiled so broadly. "I have brought you, sir, a woman of rare report."

The Governor-General looked past Deuberry. "So like him," he murmured. "A copy of the father—her forehead, the dimples of her chin and cheek, the very mould and frame of eye, nose, lips. But her beauty, scratched with briers. She has a scar across her face." He closed the door, tamped out the tobacco in his pipe, then turned to address Deuberry. "How many times has she been raped?"

"No need to ask—look at the wariness of everything about her. The scars on her face and arms."

The Governor-General motioned for Deuberry to follow him down the stairs where 'Cus and Perdita still wandered in the ante-chamber.

"What do you know of your parentage?" the Governor-General began.

Perdita didn't answer at first. Then she extracted an exotic pendant from a sack tied around her waist. Deuberry could see the Governor-General's eyes widen at the sight of it.

"The Egyptian dioptra," said the Governor-General, reverently.

Perdita touched a spring and the device opened into a circular plate divided into 360 degrees. A superbly constructed miniature pivoting alidade rode the circular plate, and equally miniature sight vanes at either end allowed the user to measure distances and angles by visual inspection of landmarks.

The Governor-General nodded. "First made by Heron of Alexandria, one of the world's greatest engineers. Do you mind if I take a closer look?"

Perdita looked inquiringly at 'Cus, who looked

inquiringly at Deuberry. At Deuberry's nod, Perdita placed the device into the Governor-General's outstretched palm.

"It's basically a theodolite. Kind of like a compass." The Governor-General pointed to an engraving along one edge of its circular border. "The inscription reads 'Hermione.'"

"I thought it might be her." Perdita tilted her head to one side as she spoke.

The Governor-General handed the pendant back to Perdita, then jerked his chin toward 'Cus. "Who is he to you?"

"Autolycus is my friend."

"That is as may please your father," said the Governor-General.

Perdita threw back her head. "I don't give a shit what my father thinks." The words rang loud and clear and seemed to reverberate against the vaulted ceiling.

The Governor-General leapt from his chair and paced to the fireplace, his back to the couple. Deuberry hurried over to him.

"She is as backward of her breeding as she is forward in her birth. She exhibits no manners, no refinement. Leo is going to have apoplexy."

"Fear none of this, for Leo's heir is found. We owe Leo nothing. Leo deserves this."

The Governor-General nodded, looked at the pair again and sighed. "Do you think either of them can read?"

"She lacks instructions, but she seems not without understanding."

Perdita approached them from behind, and spoke

in a much quieter voice, almost like a frightened girl. "I cannot speak so well, nothing so well. I mean better."

Deuberry turned. "Well, my lady, I love the cacique and through him what is nearest to him, which is your gracious self, so please embrace my direction. I'll point you to where you shall receiving clothing as shall become your highness."

The Governor-General put a hand on her shoulder. "My letters will announce you. Both of you." He nodded to 'Cus, who clapped his hands to his mouth. "Methinks I see Leontes opening his arms, weeping his welcome forth, and asking your forgiveness."

—⚉—

In the royal palace in Port au Prince, Leo took Perdita by one hand. "Is this the daughter of a king?"

Leo spared a glance at his one-time friend, the Governor-General, thinking how estranged, *en réalité* they all looked with the passage of time. The Governor-General, massaging a much greyer handlebar mustache. His own complexion now ravaged with deep wrinkles. And Perdita fairly bristled with hostility in his presence.

She wore a high-necked blouse held in place with little hooks and eyes; her hair was straightened with a hot comb and arranged Gibson Girl-style.

Nonetheless, the quality of her life was perfectly evident in the calluses he felt in her hand. And through the eyelets of the blouse, ropes of scars were visible across her shoulders, ropes that didn't look like they came to an end when the eyelets no longer opened as widely. While Leo took her hand, Perdita, stiff of posture, held her head to one side so that the scar on her face was prominently displayed.

Leo knew what she meant to convey. It was a rebuke delivered without words, as clear as if she'd slapped him across the face. What could he say? *I didn't mean for you to be sold as a slave, but to die instead, from exposure?* His daughter looked like his replica, yet was covered with scars. She conveyed nothing of his charming angel of a wife.

"I wish your mother were here."

The Governor-General took a step toward them. "Why don't we go to see the statue?"

"Can we?" Perdita finally spoke aloud, now with the longing of zealous affection.

"There we shall sup," said Leo briskly, clapping his hands for a messenger to run to Mambo's sanctuary.

When they walked in, samba music sounded softly from one side, and from the other side, the statue stood within its glass shrine.

"Masterly done," said the Governor-General, "they say one would speak to her and stand in hope of answer."

"It comes something near her natural posture." Leo spoke to Perdita, while depressing the lever. "Thus she stood, even with such life of majesty, warm life, when I first wooed her! Oh royal piece, there's magic in thy majesty. But yet," he turned to Paulina with a frown, for he'd not seen the sculpture with its veil lifted, "Hermione was not so much wrinkled, nothing so aged as this seems."

Perdita slipped through the open door, and knelt at its pedestal. "Lady, dear queen, that ended when I began."

She continued to stare and her brow furrowed, in a way that drew Leo's eyes to the statue's face.

"*Mon Pere*, would you not deem it breathed? And that those veins did *en réalité* bear blood?"

Following her gaze, Leo saw something, and felt a surge of adrenaline. "Her eye has motion in it," he yelped, wondering at the same time if it was only art playing tricks on him.

Paulina gestured to the drummers, who started a three-sixteenth rhythm.

"'Tis time, Hermione," said Paulina. "Sleep no more. Strike all that look upon you with marvel."

The statue, on its pedestal, abruptly rolled on wheels out of the glass enclosure, causing everyone to move backward. It not only rolled by itself, but moved its arms and fingers with tiny motions, like a toy doll from an amusement park. With every motion, little whining sounds, like springs in a mattress, echoed inside the chamber.

"What madness is this?" cried the Governor-General, running to the other side of Mambo's room.

'Cus clung to the walls of the sanctuary, as if staring at a ghost. Only Perdita stood close.

"Do not shun her," barked Paulina. "Present your hand."

Leo, transfixed with a strange horror, felt Paulina take his hand.

"Did you think Voudon was about death?"

"She's warm!" Leo backed away as the creature reached for his neck.

"When she was young, you woo'd her," Paulina

growled in exasperated tones. "Now in age is she to become the suitor?"

What sort of warm zombie placed its arms tenderly around one's neck? Leo wondered, confused. "If she pretends to life, let her speak." Leo watched her face intently, his heart racing, for signs of a 'living death.'

"Aye, and make manifest where she has lived, or how stolen from the dead," said the Governor-General, who sounded as if he was lost in a treacherous part of New Orleans.

"She is living, her soul white as a newborn babe," said Paulina. "Young lady, kneel and pray your mother's blessing. Behold, good lady. Our Perdita is found."

Leo was not convinced, *en réalité*. The eyes were uncanny—irises composed out of circular gear-like components, the head canting to and fro. What if 'it' bore some sort of demented consciousness not related to Hermione? Its perspective on life not the same as ours?

It seemed to settle on Perdita, and roll toward her of its own accord. Then it spoke in a strange, mechanical voice. "You Loa, look down and from your sacred vials pour your graces upon my daughter's head!"

Tears the size of junebugs rolled from Perdita's eyes.

"The last thing I remember was worrying about you, *cheri*." Hermione seemed to sway precariously for a moment before finding balance. "Anne Bolyen didn't have the opportunity to raise her daughter, nor to mend her relationship with her husband."

Hermione reached for Perdita's hand, placed it in Leo's hand, and covered them with her own. She looked into Perdita's face. Leo could see the curious mechanical eyeballs focusing.

Perdita pulled out the pendant and addressed Hermione in a small voice. "Why a compass, *Maman*?"

"Ah." Hermione reached to hold the mechanical piece with her mechanical fingers. "The dioptra. More than a compass. It helps find the fine line between two positions. It can be a guide, an aid in negotiating difficult terrain. Even," she paused, a strained mechanical expression dancing on lips not yet used to smiling, "the terrain of life and death." She canted her head to one side, toward the *Trouvé* fire. "The Yoruba people once lived in Egypt, thousands of years ago, and had to negotiate a way of life between other cultures. Even when taken to the new world, the Yoruba people were required to find the lines of demarcation between cultures. The Bokor make sure that the secrets of Heron live on, here in Haiti, but not places remote enough for a babe counted lost forever. I gave it up so you could find your way." She put the dioptra back into Perdita's hands. "Wear it well."

—⚋—

Leo ordered a private supper for eight, his guests: Hermione, the Governor-General, Deuberry, Perdita, 'Cus, with an extra place set at the chair next to Paulina for an absent Antigonus. Leo called for the band to play "After the Ball," and gestured to his daughter for a dance.

"*Mon Pere*," she said, "it's such an old tune."

"Baba," murmured Leo, making a head motion for Deuberry to offer his arm to Paulina. "It was the most popular tune in the world, in its day."

By the time the strains of the '...many a heart is aching ...,' rang out, Leo struggled to teach Perdita a waltz, Deuberry whirled Paulina around, the Governor-General turned Hermione around on her wheels, and 'Cus seemed deeply engrossed at the bench next to the piano player.

Over the sounds of the music came an inquiring knock on the double French doors. Before the security detail could move, Paulina called out. But a second voice sounded out over hers, terrible with urgency and anger.

"Do not open that door!" cried Leo.

The guards froze. The music faltered.

"A thousand knees," said Leo, looking around, Perdita in his arms, his queen paces away, his best friend and best servant nearby, "ten thousand years, naked, fasting, upon a barren mountain, and still winter in storm perpetual, could not move the gods to look that way thou wert."

Paulina stepped away from Deuberry and motioned the group to the window overlooking the courtyard. Reeling off an *ileke* necklace from around her neck, she crushed it, placed it in the candles until it glowed with fire, and tossed the embers out the window as a cloud of dust. When the dust settled to the ground, a set of footprints were illuminated, phosphorus green, leading from the doorway down the steps and into the underbrush.

"Umph, umph, umph," said Paulina. "An *Abiku* from Africa. A malignant spirit. A Bokor's ancient enemy." She slammed the window firmly. "Insatiable," she said before wiping her hands clean of crushed *ileke*. "Old as time."

Then she let out a breath like a benediction and gestured for the orchestra to proceed. "What's gone and what's past help should be past grief."

"A woman's face with artist's sure hand painted"
by J.H. Ashbee

A woman's face with artist's sure hand painted
Hast thou, the mecha-mistress of our passion;
A brazen clockwork heart, one not acquainted
With shifting change as is flesh women's fashion;
An eye as bright as theirs, though false in making,
Gilding the object whereupon it falleth;
And those of all, all hues are for your taking:
Thou steal men's eyes and certain souls appaleth.
For Sapphic woman wert thou first created,
Till cruel age brought a slow end to her breathing;
And your addition leaves me undefeated
Since the one thing added was above no-thing.
And since she pricked thee out for women's pleasure,
Both myself and my wife share in your treasure.

The Misfiring Love-Piston of Sir John Autumnrod
by Larry Kay

(Containing the conclusion of the War Between the States, and the Second Assassination of Lincoln the First)

The wide, cobbled streets of Vicksburg allowed all comers, all lovers, dusty soldiers and harried tradeswomen, dribbling automata, and dirty children chasing dogs. Even closed windows could not shut out the clopping hooves and the crackling trolleys.

However, the clang-clang of the mechanical monkey's cymbals sliced through even this din. The mustachioed news grinder cranked his wagon as the internal gadgetry selected the disc shipped direct from Washington.

A beautiful mulatto woman whispered to her parasol and miniature mechnology spun and buzzed; she wanted this recorded for her children. The steamsmith's apprentice set down the busted boiler; he knew the man whose heart it would enclose would not notice the dust.

Between them, Sir John Autumnrod, a bursting

dirigible of a man stuffed into a pair of boots better suited to a vaudeville act, waved his beret at the flies. He scratched the chafed flesh at his neck that rubbed against the new voice-box, and adjusted the heavy saber at his hip. Just then, something in him loudly failed to pass muster, flatulence or a slipping pressure relief valve—possibly both.

"Lord have mercy, man," said the lady. "Have that seen to."

"I'm a veteran, ma'am," said Autumnrod. "To be assailed by the miasma of my mechanicals is an honor many a lass has fought for."

The soot-faced youth snickered while the lady grimaced and stood off a pace. Charged and ready, the mech-monkey's eyes opened, and its speakers blared out the traditional opening: "Open your ears when loud Rumor speaks."

Autumnrod leaned forward; his ears, ringing with cannon shot from ten thousand battles, were not what they once were.

The mech-monkey grated, "I speak about General Hooker's victory…"

The monkey's master halted the recording for applause, but bold Autumnrod stole the silence and shouted, "Over a night's satin field of brothels!"

Autumnrod soaked in the laughter and ignored the news operator's snarl. Hooker's command was widely known for laying down pleasure more than taking up arms.

A well-dressed gentleman shook his fist. "Let the monkey speak, ye daft crankcase!"

Autumnrod rattled his saber. "I shall not be

slandered on this ball of earth, sir."

The man o'business relented, but so did Autumnrod, and the operator cranked the automata again. "Hooker... who in a bloody field by Chancellorsville... hath beaten down that hotspur, Stonewall Jackson, and his Rebels... nigh quenching the flame of bold rebellion!"

The steamsmith's boy rubbed his sparse chin. "Every minute now should be the father of some new stratagem."

The lady nodded. "The times are wild. The Summer of '63 shall be long remembered."

The crowd closed in for more, but the heat and humidity of Vicksburg is doom to gears and pistons. The monkey sputtered and failed, while the operator cursed. Once more, Autumnrod distinguished thunder for the thieving. He sauntered into the clearing not a pace off of the news vendor, and fingered his larynx for maximum volume.

"Rumor's tongue brings smooth-comforts-false, worse even then true-wrongs." Sir John's throat crackled and popped with static as he ignored the few jeers in the crowd.

Autumnrod threw his arms up. "List! Stonewall's 'Father,' the old Virginian, Lee, lies crafty still and marches toward Gettysburg."

Whispers sailed through the crowd, and Autumnrod surreptitiously stoked his boiler while folks gathered together. "And Major Pemberton, who is worse to us good river folk than malaria, lurks nearby ready to prove his Southern steel."

The operator cried out in victory as his mech-monkey awoke, but it only spat out, "now you have… learned from… Rumor's Tongue," and died.

Autumnrod waved the news grinder away. "Forget the official spinning disc, and hearken to me. I was there, I saw it true. I came here direct from battle."

A freed slave, proud in his bearing, stood forth. "If the battle be not fought, nor followed, nor fairly won, you tell it, then."

Another man scoffed. "Saw you the field? Came you from Chancellorsville? How be you here, metal belly, if you followed the battle? It is but days old."

Autumnrod adjusted his pistol and his saber once more so that all men would note it. "I ran from Chancellorsville, my noble sir, where hateful death put on his ugliest mask to fright our party."

Nearby, a youthful swain poked at his mate. "I think this'un ran *before* the battle."

The doubter asked, "I can see your body rife with brass, but your legs are flesh, I think. How is't you ran so far, so fast?"

"My limbs being enraged with grief were thrice themselves." Autumnrod knocked at the hard metal of his belly. "Moreover, I've lost intestines to the bayonet, and if I were to remove my fancy boots, you'd see the steel toe I have. The old one wore out kicking knaves in the arse who ask too many questions."

Laughter silenced the one man, but another partisan said, "Enough about your gewgaws. Speak on the battle."

This time Autumnrod dialed down the amplification on his voice-box, and all present leaned in as he spoke. "So did the Rebs, heavy in Jackson's loss, bend their weight. Such lightness was their fear that musket balls fled not swifter toward their aim than did the brave Rebs aiming their bayonets."

The same partisan, now backed by two more, asked, "How say you brave? Are you a Rebel-lover, then?"

Autumnrod had forgotten why he had come to Vicksburg. It was a town where deals could be carved, but it was a fickle sort, liberated by both sides more than once. Without much ado, shouts erupted and myriad devotees for North or South set to violence. Autumnrod showed the survivor's skill and slipped away.

Finally, Sir John espied a friend, his own squire at last, a scrawny girl with a permanent bemusement stuck to her face.

Watching her master flee, the squire observed, "Rebellion divides spirit from flesh, and tailor against blacksmith."

"True that, girl. We bestride a bleeding town, and must find a quick exit."

Autumnrod followed the rabbit-quick girl as she led him toward the back alleys close to the river. The Mississippi in summer did not cool them, but neither did it throw rocks.

Autumnrod wheezed and let off some pressure from his boiler. "What says... hoosh... the vizier... of my mechanical parts?

Her pony-tail bobbing, the squire shook her head in mock-seriousness. "He says the oil itself was a healthy fluid, but the party that owned it: he might have more diseases than he knew for."

Autumnrod frowned. "So, I am not only witty

myself, but the cause of wit in others?"

The squire shrugged at his displeasure, but Sir John was already distracted by some bolt or buckle that had snapped off his metal carapace. Autumnrod found the offending bit and screwed it back into place; it did not stop the deep rattle of his innards. "If Grant has put thee into my service just to set me off, thou sewer-mouthed varlet, then I will render neither silver nor gold unto you, but dress you in vile apparel and send you back again."

The squire coughed and looked away. She thought, *As I am bathed in your own stink, I think I am clothed in vile apparel already.*

Autumnrod straightened his clothes to hide the bulge of his boiler. "The good doctor may keep his own grace, but he is out of mine." The squire waited obediently for instruction. "What said Master Dombledon, about the fluid for my poor piston? That sublime valve has not worked proper in a fortnight. The women of Vicksburg cry every night, I assure thee."

With a bluntness, the squire said, "He'll not take your credit."

"Credit?! I would sooner put saltpeter in my furnace than stand on credit with any man." Autumnrod spat a great oily glob into the river. "Where's Barfled?"

"He's gone to buy your worship a horse."

"Good; I intend to be lubed, drained, horsed, and whored by the end of this day."

"We kill two birds with one purchase then?"

Autumnrod let fly a hard hand, but his deft squire ducked, and the matter was dropped. As the mismatched duo slipped through byways and over stinking canals, a pair of men known to the same back alleys finally caught up to them.

The squire said, "Sirrah, it is the law. Run off and I'll tell them a tale."

"Too late, girl. Pray tell him my audio is failing."

"But your ears are flesh, sir."

"I am deaf from perturbations of the brain," said Sir John, who then turned away, affecting a deep thinker's stare into the distance.

As the two lawmen approached, the squire said with all innocence, "My master is deaf, sirs."

The old sheriff stuck his thumbs in his pants and sighed heavily. "I am sure he is, to the hearing of anything good. Go pluck him by the elbow. I must speak with him."

Autumnrod, seeing his gambit failed, tossed his own question first. "Have you news of Grant?"

The sheriff cast a glance at the rushing ooze of the sewers. "He nears, though slowly."

Autumnrod nodded as if he knew the mind of all high men. "I hear he has a lethargy of the blood."

The sheriff scowled. "And you have contracted this as well, I see."

"Heaven forefend. My means are thin but my waist is grand. I suffer not at all."

"Not so. If infamy be a disease, then you have that to be sure."

"How can you say this to my teeth?"

The sheriff smoothed his enormous silver mustachio. "There have been complaints: your night's exploit on Gads-hill."

Autumnrod fought off a smile. "Surely, no one with

a name in the daylight would complain of my visits in the night, Old Stash. Do not measure the heat of our livers with the bitterness of your gall."

The sheriff spat. "Think you a young swain, then, with your grey beard, your protruding furnace, your broken voice? Every part about you is blasted with antiquity." The deputy by the sheriff's side smirked around his chewing tobacco.

Sir John rapped on his bulk. "Fie! Inside this rusted carcass beats a bull's heart. Just this last week I had a new Dionysus 200 filter installed to replace my liver."

The sheriff smiled like the trickster fox. "That is good to hear, Sir John. For I have the power in me to invest a virile knight such as yourself to marshal forth and sweat Lee at Gettysburg."

One of Autumnrod's gaskets burped. "I spake too soon. I need oil first." His squire was about to say something, but Autumnrod clapped a hand on her. "As a veteran, I need to lead men into battle. Can you lend me a hundred dollars from the treasury to furnish me forth?"

"Not a penny." The sheriff tipped his hat. "Heaven bless your expedition. I'll hearken to the sound of your glories on the next rumor-monkey's disc." Both lawmen left.

Autumnrod snarled at them. "What money is in my purse, girl?"

"Confederate or Union paper?"

"Whatever serves."

"Seven dollars and change at best." She looked him over as a butcher might a cow. "Enough coin to fix some disease... or gather more."

Autumnrod hissed as if breached. "I don't know which poxy is worse, your vulgar tongue or the leprosy of my purse." The squire pretended to stuff an errant twirl of hair behind her ear. Sir John rubbed his beard. "I must make friends with speed. Never so few, yet more in need. First, send a letter to Grant. Tell him the how the city seethes and ask him for a position in his Army of Tennessee that is for such as me."

"I will counsel every man for the aptest way for safety. Pray continue."

Autumnrod did not pause to challenge her subtle claim of cowardice. "And a post to old Mistress Ursula, whom I have weekly sworn to marry, since I perceived the first white hair on my chin. Go!"

Sir John watched his squire salute, smirk, and run off with his posts. "A good wit will make use of anything: I will turn disease to commodity."

—⚍—

Grant's camp flowed in as much color and disarray as the nearby river. Only the shoddy vittles and the endless cleaning of the static cannons remained the same from camp to camp. Pale youths danced an Irish jig as a dark-complected trumpeter played them on. It eased Grant's mind to see the squads mix. He had not thought the races could get along, but the war had proved him wrong. He was glad of it.

Grant put down the soup of boiled cabbage, and shook a spoon at the commander at his arm. "Lieutenant, we have failed over water five times to crack this Gibraltar of the Confederacy."

"Aye, sir. Lady Vicksburg taunts us from her high hill."

"I shall be forced to more boldness over land. You have heard our causes and know our means. My most noble Lieutenant, I pray you, speak plainly your opinions of our hopes."

"We survive only on the charity of the slaves in the nearby plantations."

Grant stroked his unkempt beard. "Thank God for them. We line ourselves with hope, eating the air, on promise of supply."

The Lieutenant, clean-shaven and without humor, said, "Pemberton's men, who we chase, are worse off. They eat their shoes by now, I'll warrant."

"Rebs." Grant rubbed at something caught in his teeth. "They think to pluck the Union down, but their body is not strong enough to equal Lincoln even in his sickbed."

"Aye, sir." The Lieutenant gazed off at a squad of men cursing at a failed static charger. "Have we allies in Vicksburg? Perhaps our black regiments may know a few bodies in that town."

Grant spat out a foul dollop of canteen water. "I know of one who would be handy if it comes to siege."

The Lieutenant hid his pinched face. "Please, tell me, sir, you do not mean Sir John Autumnrod. Your love for that evil angel turns Lincoln against you."

"I have drawn steel with him and eaten at his table. You say give him up?"

"You promised Lincoln you'd give up strong drink and the vulgar hearts that would pour it down your gullet. Autumnrod is midwife to lechery."

"He has saved my life aplenty."

"I tell you he wounds it now."

Grant turned his eye to the muddy Mississippi. It would be so easy to grab a steamer and find Glutton John and his roustabouts. They could all go west and sun-dance with the Dakota, or take an airship north and shoot beaver with the Cree. Why did great men have to keep foisting command on him?

General Grant sighed, and adjusted the prisms on the spyglass. He could almost count Major Pemberton's buttons. If only his sharpshooters were the equal of his scope.

At his side, his Lieutenant grunted. "We've attacked Pemberton twice and have only driven him into the trenches."

Grant winced at the truth. "I know his honor. He will dig in like a chigger about Vicksburg though he knows it makes poor sense."

"Lee could use him at Gettysburg."

Grant nodded. "And I, though we outnumber him two to one, will give siege though I know it is folly. God willing I should be with Meade's Army of the Potomac and crush Lee in a vise."

The Lieutenant asked, "Shall I send runners into the city and see what flavor they wear this week?"

"The only flavor I would care to know is which small beer they favor and whence it might flow upon mine lips. I am exceeding weary."

The Lieutenant dropped his voice. "Is it come to that, sir? I had thought weariness durst not have attached to your flesh."

"My appetite is not princely. I know Lincoln would

chide me for it, but the yearning for it discolors my complexion."

The Lieutenant unnecessarily smoothed his jacket. "Have you heard from Lincoln? Has he recovered from his fell wounding?"

Grant tried to rub at the pain behind his eyes. "His spirit's strength shames me. I fear it will leave his flesh, and fly straight here to set more cares upon my brow. Yet I tell thee, my heart bleeds inwardly, that the nation's Father is so sick."

The Lieutenant stifled a grin. "You are not so far in the Devil's Book as some would say."

Grant assayed the lines of men against him, and the camp of men and women behind him. Their suffering pressed on his brow and dried his mouth. "And you are right, let us send a man to assay the city."

A young messenger, her hair short like a boy's, stopped her run to report. "From the city, a squire and a lieutenant to see you, sir."

The General and the Lieutenant grinned at their good fortune.

Barfled walked over, saluted. "Your Grace."

Grant clapped arms with the man. "Well met, kindly Barfled. And the girl that I gave Sir Autumnrod. He had her from me Christian, and see if the fat villain hath not transformed her Ape."

The squire said nothing and Barfled did not argue. "Deliver your letter and be gone, Rabbit."

The squire, all business in posture, but mockingly so when addressing Barfled, said, "I shall, Master." She handed a letter to Grant. "Perhaps I'll find a stew nearby that I can improve by jumping in it." She turned smartly and left.

Barfled jerked his thumb over his shoulder. "If you do not make her be hanged among you, the gallows shall be wronged."

The Lieutenant sneered. "It is Autumnrod's influence."

Grant opened the letter and read aloud. "'I, Sir John Autumnrod, Captain of Brave Men and Knight to Lincoln's favored military son, General Grant, give greetings.' Hmmm. After the flattery, he talks about the city, and Pemberton's forces, and his own."

The Lieutenant's face scrunched in puzzlement. "He commands a company of men?"

Barfled looked away. "He gathers them as we speak, from Eastcheap to Oldchurch."

Grant grinned and clapped Barfled's shoulder. "I think he gathers amongst women such as a bey has a harem, and dines on every pleasure from sweet smoke to soft caresses. Would that I were a shadow to slip up on him."

The Lieutenant, his face dark with irritation, said, "Would that I could follow you. I would steep this letter in sherry and make him eat it."

Grant patted his belly. "I like that thought, too."

The Lieutenant acted as if a priest had peed on him. "Remember Lincoln's shade, Your Grace. He would favor you for the presidency if you only forsook your love of small beer and wild company."

Grant turned back to the horizon and the enemy hunkering down for the coming weeks of privation. If only privation did not seek him out as well.

The Inn of Good Cheer shook with laughter as one of the metal Immaculata fell to the floor and upturned a table, two men, and one barmaid with it. While it was disputed in some circles as to whether the automatic men had a soul, it was without question that they suffered, and in suffering found spiked ethanol.

"Gear-blasted fool can't hold his liquor," said the Hostess to Doll. "If the tin bastard fires up that disc on polkas again, I'll have him rusticated with extreme prejudice."

Doll shrugged as three dock hands returned the auto-man to his chair, where he attempted to perform a shaky surgery on a busted servo-mechanism in his fourth arm.

Doll, serene in her lace undergarments, perched on the bar, and blew delicate hexagons of blue smoke. She had bought the ingenious pipe from a Chinese dealer to add to her careful appearance of unworldly beauty. A wobbling man, already half out of his clothes, approached her with a leering intent to possess that beauty.

Doll sighed at the sweaty man's progress. "Can an empty vessel bear such a huge hog's head? If you love me, Hostess, you'll fill my glass with your best red."

The Hostess complied, but whispered, "Go you easy on the wine. It does more than give you color."

Doll eyed her reflection in the bar-length mirror. "Aye, it perfumes my blood."

The flimsy doors to the bawdy house swung open with a bang. Autumnrod sauntered in and placed his hands on his hips. "I am Arthur returned. Who shall find a sheath for Excalibur?"

The crowd hushed at this potential new entertainment. Doll pushed the beslobbering local man off her. She pitched her voice to command the room. "Not Arthur. Thou art but an oil-dribbling Mordred at best."

Autumnrod smiled. "My pike bent bravely, true, but I to surgery bravely, too; and so return to venture upon the charged chambers bravely presented here. My piston's well oiled, and my boiler's fired hot."

Doll puffed out figure-eights from her pipe. "I think you mistake pressure for passion, sir. Look, Hostess. There's a whole merchant's venture in him."

The Hostess stage-whispered to Doll: "I have not seen a hulk better stuffed in the hold." Then to Sir John: "You'll need servos with stamina to satisfy the mechanical marvel under her skirts."

"Oh, aye, Hostess. Aye, Doll. I may have coin, and sausage pie, and a roof from Mistress Ursula, but only your shiny portcullis can handle my pneumatic love."

Doll pointed her pipe at John's groin. "Thou art a mechanical horror, Sir John Brokenrod. I think you must barter with the Immaculata here for the unspoken love."

The auto-man's hind rotors buzzed at the reference. It said, "Sir John knows my receivers too well, Mistress Doll. I still need repairs from his last visit."

"Am I, a veteran, to be turned away from all pleasure?" Autumnrod downed the lager offered him and gestured for another. He sauntered up to Doll.

Doll slipped a hand into his shirt and tapped the furnace's gauge. "The war calls you back, my brave warrior. If you must have it quick, swagger out to the train yard… and rub thy swagger on the engines there."

The Immaculata's voicebox crackled. "You two never meet, but you fall to verbal blows."

Doll and John exchanged smoldering, amused glances. Before either could continue, a commotion outside stole Autumnrod's attention. He returned to the door, and cheered. He announced to the inn: "For am I not the Pendragon? It is my table round of knights."

"I'll have no swaggering companions of yours," shouted the Hostess, "if they trade on cheap talk and empty purses."

Barfled and the squire entered, both with a wary eye as if mugs might be thrown at them. The local drunk, taking advantage of the lull, grabbed at Doll.

Doll pushed him back. "I scorn you, base linen-mate. Away."

The swaying man struggled to stay on his feet. "I know your ways and means. Don't throw airs at me, whore."

Doll showed her teeth in a fierce grin. "I'll thrust my knife in your moldy chaps, lack-wit, if you play the saucy cuttle with me."

The blindly determined man drew steel and made it two steps before Autumnrod appeared at his side. Without a word, Sir John bashed the man in the head, and he dropped. Autumnrod grinned until the man's brother spun him about and planted a solid fist into Sir John's chin. John wavered while Barfled, with the speed of a mech-assisted veteran, sent the man to the floor with a practiced hammerblow.

Doll leapt down to hoist Autumnrod toward the

table with the auto-man. She asked, "Are you hurt? Is your pike bravely bent again?"

Autumnrod waved for a drink. "He was a rascal to try me. Love to you, Barfled."

Barfled shrugged while Doll brushed John's mane of hair into a semblance of order. "You sweet knight, let me wipe your face. We will weld thine heavenly frame back together."

"Peace, good Doll, do not speak like a deathshead."

Ethanol, red wine, and dearest rum followed and flowed. And flowered such fellow feeling that the inn earned its name thrice-fold. Song and dance livened the night, and even the Hostess was convinced to dance a polka from the auto-man's collection.

Unnoticed, two men in rain cloaks entered and took a table.

"I think that bearded fellow there is known to me," said Autumnrod, squinting at the newcomers.

The Hostess, perhaps wishing to avoid another fight, gestured at Doll.

Doll cooed in Autumnrod's ear, "I'll canvas thee between a pair of sheets, Sir John. The night grows late, and I haven't been plucked all night."

Doll led Autumnrod to a private booth, no more than a partition of silk, but enough for the rough sensibilities of the Inn of Good Cheer. Before long, a spastic jack-hammering assaulted the ear, to be followed by the strained hiss of escaping steam.

Grant's Lieutenant cringed at the aural spectacle. "Strange that Desire should so many years outlive Performance."

"Who said that?" Autumnrod, a spent wreck of

mussed clothing and oil-stained metalwork, erupted from his conjugal cloister.

Everyone present stared over at the table with the two new arrivals. Autumnrod did nothing to make his appearance more seemly as he bounded over to accost his insulters. He stopped when he saw them.

"You look like my old rum-fellow, Ulysses Grant."

"I've heard I have a resemblance to the man," said Grant quietly.

The Lieutenant, full ready to bare his blade, sneered at Sir John and leaned back to show he wore steel. "Look, if the withered Elder hath not his pole clawed like a Parrot."

Autumnrod frowned away the Lieutenant's presence, and stared at the seated man through his fog of liquor. "Aha. I know that you are not him because your hands are empty, sir. Grant would have a mug in each hand and a girl on his knee."

Grant's face remained stony. "You seem to know him well."

"He was ever my shadow. I tutored him in my own philosophies, but he has fallen from my teachings. His wit is thick like mustard without me." A few jeers erupted from the crowd and Sir John warmed to his point. "When Grant was naked, he was like a forked radish." Autumnrod soaked in the laughter now, blind to the grim duo before him. "He came ever in the rearward of the fashion. Indeed, I saved Grant from his own cowardice more than once."

Grant placed a steadying hand on the Lieutenant, and the other man returned to his seat.

Autumnrod tugged at his clothing like any politician

on the stump, no matter it lay in tatters about his boiler. "And even though I could never wear a smooth boot, I swear I live in his good grace. The general will pay me back for my many kindnesses when Lincoln dies."

"Is he so sick?" asked Grant with downcast eyes, barely letting the words come forth.

Autumnrod waved his torn cravat in the air. "If not this bullet, then another. The man attracts them and canst barely duck with his great height. Grant will rise when Lincoln falls, and Sir John Autumnrod will rise with him."

Grant stood then, but Autumnrod failed to see it as Doll, coifed and smooth again, if in high color, emerged from the booth. She asked, "When you rise to heights, what will you buy for me?"

Autumnrod swung his arm as if to encompass the world. "A cape and a cap and a song. I will sing it for you e'en now."

Grant, with the voice that commanded good men to die horribly, spoke: "I have a different song for you, Sir John Autumnrod of the Wicked House."

Autumnrod turned at the interruption to see the two men standing, displeased in face, stern in posture. The Lieutenant said, "You see before you not the semblance of Grant, but the General himself. How now your insults?" And then to the inn at large: "Where is your merriment now?"

The crowd, from barmaid to hostess to auto-men, stared open-mouthed at the spectacle before them. Doll's hand covered her mouth.

Autumnrod paled, clutched at his clothing, but could not command his faculties. "I think... I am too deep in sherry."

Grant grabbed his coat. "I think you have warned me off drink by your deepness in it. Even Lee in his camp of sworn foes does not yearn for Lincoln's death like you do. I have seen the truth of your villainy. I am late to be quit of it."

Autumnrod, finally waking to his doom, tried to spin gold from hay. "I–I but dispraised Lincoln before the Wicked, that the Wicked might not fall in love with him. In which doing, I have done the part of a careful friend, and–and a true subject."

Grant shrugged into his coat and pointed at Autumnrod like a preacher. "Fie on thee and thy churlish tongue. Say no more. Even now I must return to the Tempest of Commotion. All present should pray that Lincoln survives the cowardly iron in his chest."

Grant and his Lieutenant left the silent inn. Sir John stumbled back into the booth where he had just reached such highs, and rubbed his head in confusion. Around him, whispers, blown by surmises, jealousies, and conjectures, sprouted uncounted heads, and slithered into the night.

—⚘—

President Lincoln lay in bed surrounded by clicking, whirring, and humming machines. He did not mind their constant buzz, for if they stopped, so would he. However, he did mind the cables, pistons, gears, manifolds, and blowers that represented his current insides, for they chafed and stank, and made his every waking hour like something from Dante's nightmares.

His iconic hat sat atop a deactivated auto-man at the far end of his chamber. The a-man was meant to be his butler and guard, but it allowed its boiler to cool at night at Lincoln's request. The dying president liked to talk to himself, and he did not want to be recorded, even by his most intimate automata.

"How many of my countrymen are at this hour adrift in the arms of nature's soft nurse? How I must fright thee, Sleep, with my bronze guts, that thou wilt no more weigh my eye-lids down."

The President's aides knocked on his chamber door. He could tell it was Abner by the tiny, insistent rap.

Abner entered like a penitent monk. "How now, sir?"

Barstow, his nephew, followed behind, trying to cheer the dim room with his bright, open face.

Lincoln pushed himself up on the thick pillows. "Uneasy lies the head that wears the crown. I feel the Union's struggles even as my makeshift heart sputters." Lincoln fiddled with the hissing contraption nearest him while his aides gathered their courage enough to speak.

Barstow nodded. "Many good-morrows to your Majesty."

Lincoln gestured them come close. "Is it a good morrow? You perceive the body of our nation, how foul it is, what rank diseases grow, what danger nears the heart?"

Abner spared a glance at his nephew at such dour speech. Did Lincoln talk of the nation or his own flesh? Finally, the senior aide mumbled, "As a body, the

Union is yet distempered—"

Barstow laid a hand on his uncle's stooped shoulder. "—Which to its former strength may be restored. With good advice, and little medicine, the Old Virginian will soon be cooled."

Lincoln stared at the expensive clockwork mechanism on his side table; it irised every sixteen minutes. It held the chromatograph of his beloved Mary, dead these eight months after taking a bullet meant for him. He said, "O heaven, that one might read the book of Fate, and see the revolution of the times."

The aides shifted in place, and bowed their heads as if Lincoln recited a prayer.

Lincoln scratched at an offending tube. "'Tis not four years gone since Bobby Lee and I did feast together. Even Jackson, called now Stonewall, was once nearest my soul, and toiled in my affairs. Many fellows we now call enemy once laid love and life under my sign."

Abner nodded. "There is a history in all men's lives, sir."

Barstow said, "And weak beginnings lie entreasured, for such things become the hatch and brood of time."

Lincoln rubbed at his chest where the metal broke the flesh. "Speaking of weak beginnings, how are my generals this month?"

Both aides hesitated. Lincoln was known to curse his generals as gremlins sent to ruin the clockwork of the nation.

Lincoln's boiler pinged and knocked with sudden heat; his eyes grew grim at their hesitation. "Bull Run. Bloody Antietam. Fredericksburg. Chancellorsville. Fie on these paper warriors switched at birth for spineless automata."

Lincoln knew his tirades made his aides uncomfortable, but he could not help himself. He growled and checked the gauges for his pressure and temperature. "They say Lee marches to Gettysburg with fifty thousand strong."

Abner rubbed his hands together. "Rumor doth double, like the echo, the numbers of the feared."

Barstow gestured toward the window as if one could see the army through Lincoln's reinforced windows. "The powers that you have already sent forth shall bring this prize in very easily."

Lincoln nodded and looked over at his wife's picture again. His aides knew his manners; they left silently, the door closing with an echoing click.

"Mary, these unseasoned hours will send us all to the holy land."

—⚏—

The suffocating heat added insult to the daily grind of the sixth week of the Vicksburg siege. The Union camp, barely open to supply itself, had little to be happy about, save the fact their foes suffered more. Animals disappeared from pens, and shadows raided ill-fenced gardens. Even so, the rebels starved.

On a hill with a good view, but no real breeze, sat vigilant Grant. The Lieutenant walked up to his general with a brisker step than usual. "Sir. Our spies have born wondrous fruit. I have here intercepted letters from the Old Virginian, their cold intent, tenure, and substance."

Grant, red-eyed and weary, turned from his watch on the rebel trenches. "Read on, then."

The Lieutenant skimmed the notes, searching for the best parts. "'Led on by bloody youth, guarded with rage... countenanced by boys and beggary.' He thinks little of our Northern mettle. 'We give only ground to build a grief on.' He intends to make a stand, sir. At Gettysburg will we make Lee feel the bruises of the long days."

Grant nodded slowly. "It would be good to see an end. I have a disc from Lincoln as well."

"How is't with our nation's Father?"

"He is worn thin and dry, but hopes for a solid Union as ever. Even dying from fell Southern treachery, he will keep no tell-tale in his memory. He knows we fight kin and cannot so precisely weed this land, that plucking to unfix an enemy, he doth shake a friend."

The Lieutenant frowned at the open sympathy. "Yet many a garden is overgrown. Perhaps a military man in the presidency will have a firmer resolve against the Southern disgrace."

Grant cut his eyes to his earnest, young commander. "You make him sound a fangless lion, Lieutenant. Do not blow the trumpet of war so loud. Lincoln knows the parcels and particulars of our grief, whereon this hydra-spawn of war is born. He would drink friendly with the enemy... if only they sit at the table."

"But–"

"As would I."

"Yes, sir."

Since horses were of short supply in hungry Vicksburg, Autumnrod had traded for a steam-carriage. He could only afford the one with a faulty furnace, and so intended to connect his own boiler for the vehicle's use. His eminent logic was not conveyed to the Almighty, and his jalopy had broken down within a day's ride of Vicksburg. Unable to fix the contraption, unwilling to walk back to shame, he waited by the road on God's mercy.

A weak cloud of dust brought Sir John out of his stupor. "Perhaps it is one of my hired men returned with good news. It was sad to send them on to glory without me, but such is a leader's curse."

The cloud finally assumed the shape of a ragged man in Confederate gray. His fine boots, expensive saddle, and polished saber spoke of a gentleman, but if he was gentle-born, he was, of the nonce, misery-bred.

Autumnrod knew his only weapon was bluster since he could not ring steel, and his poor eyes would not permit a musket shot even if he had one. No matter. The bluff and the bluster, true weapons in his masterly hands, could unman a centurion. He would subdue this lonely Reb... just as soon as he rode a little closer.

Eventually, Autumnrod addressed the man with vigor. "What's your name, sir? Of what condition are you? And of what place, I pray?"

The man stopped his horse, but seemed unworried, or uncaring. "I am a captain, sir. My men called me Coleville of the Dale."

"Well then, Coleville shall still be your name, a Traitor your degree, and the Dungeon your place."

Coleville raised a brow in sudden recognition

of such heralded bombastity. "You must be Sir John Autumnrod."

"As good a man as he, sir, who ere I am. Do ye yield, sir, or shall I sweat for you? If I do sweat, they are the drops of thy lovers, and they weep for thy death. Therefore, rouse up fear and trembling, and do observance to my mercy."

Coleville moved not at all, but smiled. "I see I have met an Iron man, cheering a rout of rebels with your drum, turning the word to sword, and life to death."

"Your twice-turned words daren't even touch my blood, for I sit within a General's heart, and ripen in the sunshine of his favor."

Before Coleville could respond, a most serious cloud of dust and thunder rounded the bend. From this commotion came many suits of blue, which then resolved itself to be none other than the honor guard of General Grant himself. With muskets trained, the bristling party halted. Grant and Autumnrod caught each other's eye, but neither spoke.

Finally, the Lieutenant's scornful voice broke the hot air. "When everything is ended, then you come. These tardy tricks of yours should, one time or other, break some gallows back."

Sir John kept a remorseful eye to Grant's manner, but he would not hear disdain from any other man. "Do you think me a swallow or a musket ball? Have I, in my poor and old motion, the expedition of thought? I have speeded hither with the very extremist inch of possibility. I have sent on three score men to Gettysburg with my exhortations. And here, travel-tainted as I am, have, in my pure and immaculate valor, taken Captain

Coleville of the Dale, a most furious rebel. Indeed, I do follow the Roman way. In short: I came, saw, and over-came."

Grant, reserved in his demeanor, nodded to the Confederate officer. "More of his courtesy than your deserving."

The Lieutenant turned his horse and looked the weary Southern man over. "A famous rebel art thou, Coleville?

Autumnrod knocked his own boiler. "And a famous true subject took him."

Coleville shrugged. "What news, sirs, of the city?"

"Pemberton has seen reason. The siege is over."

"I was leading men there to relieve him. And Lee?"

No one present wanted to kick a broken man. Even as soldiers took the man's static-charges and musket, Grant gave the man a level eye. "Our reports conflict. Most say it will turn the tide."

Coleville, his fight over either way, nodded. "I hear Lincoln is sore sick."

The Lieutenant grimaced. "And now dispatch we toward the capital to be at his side."

Sir John cleared his throat. "My lord, I beseech you, when you come to capital's court, remember our shared histories in your good report."

Grant held up a hand to forestall more entreaties. "Fare you well, Autumnrod, I shall better speak of you to Lincoln than you deserve."

With that, Grant and the squad departed with Coleville in tow. Autumnrod grinned ear to ear as he was consumed by dust. Even broken down as he was, victory could still find its fickle way to his arms.

Autumnrod held forth at the Inn of Good Cheer like Mad King George. All present knew Sir John's lifetime of boasting and borrowing would finally pay off, and they were glad to be a part of it. While one of the Immaculata filled the room with clashing lights and a fine Cajun reel, Sir John, standing on a table, expostulated on his best subject.

"A good rum ascends into the brain, dries up the dull vapors, and makes it full of nimble, delectable shapes which become excellent wit."

The crowd cheered him, knocked mugs into tables, stamped their feet, and hollered for more wisdom.

"The second property of your excellent rum is the warming of the blood, for it illuminateth the face, which gives warning to villains of my rage." Autumnrod shook his saber's hilt.

"Watch out for Sir John!"

"Rum for all!

"I would give a snifter to every soul were I to run for office," said Autumnrod.

"You've got my vote," said Doll.

"Nay, love. I would run but for General Grant, who is like a brother to me, and he loves spirits high and low as I. He hath tempered his cold blood with imbibing fertile rum, by my own example, and has become hot and valiant. If I had a thousand sons, the first principle I would teach them... to be like Grant and forswear thin potations!"

The ebullient crowd carried Autumnrod's fancies long into the night.

Lincoln roved around his war room with his cane whirring and clicking on each step. An open Bible hung from his hand as he consulted the maps on every wall and table.

Abner and Barstow nearly knocked down the door with their entrance. Their faces could barely contain their triumph, as if they had fought the battles themselves instead of merely bringing news of them.

Abner nearly shouted. "Vicksburg is fallen! The Mississippi will hold no more rebel custom."

Lincoln nodded, absorbed the news, consulted the largest map that showed the mighty river choked off by Confederate colors. He said, "The Father of Waters again goes unvexed to the sea."

Barstow almost clapped such was his liveliness. "And there is other good news."

Lincoln grinned. "Well then. Let me adjust my valves."

"Lee retreats from Gettysburg. Meade has finally shaved the old lion."

Lincoln let out a long-held breath. "So. Everything lies level to our wish." He pressed at one of the cables protruding from his belly, and winced. "Only we want a little personal strength to see those rebels still afoot to come underneath the rule of the Union."

Abner glanced at the silent auto-man, and the dent it carried from a foeman's cowardly pistol. "You have survived two assassins, your Grace."

Barstow nooded vigorously. "Your brass has brought vigor to us all."

Lincoln waved away the fawning sentiments. "Does Meade pursue Lee?"

"He is consolidati–"

Lincoln slapped the table with his clockwork cane, and a piece of ornate brass flew off. It was his fourth walking stick. "Meade hesitates! He dithers when he should conquer." His aides stared at the map. "Where is wastrel Grant?" The aides looked at each other, then down. Lincoln grunted. "Grant was ever the fattest soil to weeds. When I finally slip my last gear, you here will have to deal with his head-strong riot."

Abner and Barstow murmured complimenting platitudes about Lincoln's remaining life, and his myriad generals' eventual moves toward ending the war. Lincoln leaned on the table, suddenly weak, and both men rushed to him.

"I pray you bear me hence into my bedchamber."

They assisted the president until his auto-man valet could take up the burden. Lincoln whispered to his aides, "Let there be no noise unless some favorable hand will whisper music to my weary spirit."

—⚹—

Abner and Barstow took the pneumatic elevator back down to the main floor. "Uncle, that was the best news we've had in two years, yet he rages and then goes slack. I so looked forward to seeing the worry fade from his face, and now…"

"I know, nephew. He is not like other men. These fits are, with his presidency, very ordinary. We stand from him, give him air. He'll straight be well."

"These pangs, the incessant care, and labor of his mind, Uncle... I fear if we won the war, the news would kill him."

Abner raised an instructive finger. "When we win the war, Nephew, he will surely pass the veil, but he will die with a spirit becalmed. That will do for me."

The two chief aides returned to the public rooms, and heard the news of Sherman's march through the South, punishing the Confederates for their brazen desire for secession. They argued on whether such news would fire Lincoln's boiler, or send him further into melancholy. Such was their state when Grant entered the room.

The aides shared a surprised look. Grant had been summoned, but he was ahead of schedule... and... clear-headed.

Grant asked, "How is he?"

"His eye is hollow, and he changes with the hour."

"He would see you. You could tell him of Sherman."

Grant nodded, took the elevator, and navigated the shadows of the White House until he found Lincoln's bedchamber. He did not wish to even breathe, as if such a small sound might disturb the rarefied air of the chamber. He nodded to the auto-man percolating quietly in the corner, and then sat by his president's bed. Lincoln was gray and motionless. Even his mechnology seemed cold and dead. Is this what the "throne" held for him?

The seal of the Union, the symbol they all bled for, and Lincoln wasted away for, sat on a nearby pillow. Grant picked up the seal and went to a window. "I could toss this cursed disc into the garden and see it buried. It scalds the great man more than an over-fired boiler. Why doth the seal become such a troublesome bedfellow?"

Lincoln awoke without sound, and saw Grant by the window, the seal of office in his hands. His voice sour and weak, he said, "Are you so hasty, that you doth suppose my sleep for death?"

Grant turned, his cheeks flush, his eyes wet.

Lincoln saw the tears, and nodded. "I thought for a moment that hunger lurked behind my empty chair, Ulysses."

"No, sir."

"A thousand daggers hide in my thoughts in these end days."

Grant looked down at the seal, then outside again.

Lincoln sat up fully. "Even now, with victory on the horizon, I fear the wild dogs that flesh their tooth in every innocent."

Grant turned, his face haloed by the window's light. "Even now we endeavor to knit our powers to the army of tranquility. Soon, I pray, there be not a rebel's sword unsheathed. Peace shall put forth her olive everywhere."

Lincoln's face, ever clouded, lightened at the sentiment. Grant walked slowly to the bed, knelt, and took Lincoln's hand. "Heaven witness with me, Abraham, when I here came in, and found no course of breath within your presidency... how cold it struck my heart. I wondered if I could do as you have done... to give all."

Lincoln held his hand. "I fail, 'tis plain, but you should live, and let me die, and let too the wildness in thee die as well."

Grant listened, and warmly squeezed his liege's hand. Lincoln, his coils and tubes struggling against the failing flesh, said, "By what crooked way I met this seal, and I myself know well how troublesome it sat, to thee it shall descend with even less quiet, but... better opinion, and better confirmation. How I came by the seal... O heaven forgive, and grant it may, with thee, in true peace... live."

Grant, with solemn eye, said, "My gracious Abraham, I, with uncommon pain, against all the world, will, your vision, rightfully maintain."

Lincoln sagged backward onto his pillows, but held tight to Grant's hand. "You bring happiness and peace to the hollow of my heart. Now this chamber shall be my Jerusalem. Let the coal finally burn down in my boiler. Let Lincoln die."

Grant held his president's hand as Lincoln's spirit slipped free, his gauges zeroed out, and his bellows whispered their last. After a long moment, Grant picked up the American seal again. The symbolic metal disc felt even heavier in his hands.

—⚜—

Lincoln's death was kept secret for months until it was clear Lee had given up hope for victory. The warring powers came to Appomattox, and peace left that signing hall, if not good will. The electors lauded Grant in due course. His inaugural address was carried by rumor-monkey to all quarters. In Vicksburg, they cheered loudest of all, for merriment could return to that lusty city in true. Autumnrod tossed future favor to all men who would take him to the capital, and earn his right and due from his "Friend in the House."

The colorful parade that followed the dour inauguration was the event of the decade. So the dusty, bedraggled troop of Sir John's pained the eye and assaulted the nose. As such, they were given wide berth, and had an excellent viewing stage for the festivities.

The squire poked Sir John. "Sir, would we not be better served with a shave and a bar of soap?"

Autumnrod did not even look at her, for his eye scanned the passing horses and steam-carriages for only one man. "I stand stained with travel, and sweating with desire to see our new liege. Thinking of nothing else, putting all affairs in oblivion, as if there were nothing else to be done, but to see him."

"So... no bath then."

"Away, varlet. I see his party even now."

President Grant, perhaps too closely acquainted with the death-dealing side of the newest mechnology, chose tradition, and had outfitted his carriage with only a team of black horses. A few aides and guards rode escort, half of them studiously ignoring Autumnrod and his party of ne'er-do-wells.

Autumnrod turned up his voice-box and shouted: "I would speak to thee, my President!"

The carriage came to a stop. The aides frowned, and the stiff-backed guards fingered their static-pistols. Grant opened the door and a small metal stage unfolded for him to stand on. Reporters crowded the sudden scene. Well-wishers pressed forward. The guards flexed with anxiety.

Grant spoke so all could hear. "I see thee John Autumnrod, Imp of Fame. I see the tutor and the feeder of my riots."

Autumnrod and his throng leaned backwards as one, aghast and agog at the chastisement in the president's tone. The reporters scribbled; the aides smirked.

Grant continued, "Presume not that I am the thing that I was. For heaven doth know that I have turned away from my former self."

Autumnrod was glad for the press of bodies around him, as he did not trust his knees.

Grant trained his baleful eye fully on Sir John Autumnrod. "I banish thee, on pain of death, as I have done the rest of my misleaders, not to come near our House."

Grant returned to the velvet confines of his carriage and the parade continued. Even when the long line of dignitaries ended and the crowds faded, Autumnrod could not move from the spot of his lashing.

Finally, his voice desperate and cracking, John announced, "Look you, he must seem thus... to the world. Fear not your advancement. I will yet be the man that shall make you great."

With jeers and curses, the small mob of sycophants left. Only Barfled and the squire remained to witness Sir John's grief.

—⚘—

The squire, her hair cleaned, her face washed, knelt down to the grave and propped the pneumatic piston that was Sir John Autumnrod's pride in an upright position. She stood there for a long time, waiting, perhaps, for the chill morning air to say something.

Finally, she said, "A once great warrior, who could not learn to appear more wise, and modest to the world. He who chewed life like no other, spit the seeds and let others clean the husks, lies here unmourned."

"Not unmourned," said President Grant, appearing by her side. He held a half-empty bottle of rum. "How then did he die?"

The squire paused, but could not look Grant in the face. Then: "He died in a sweat, over a night-lady."

"The grave gaped thrice wider for him than for other men."

Her jaw firmed. "Yet I think he was already killed with thine hard opinion."

"As ever, your words are like daggers."

"But you weep not."

"I have trouble finding tears for my old friend."

"Then pour yon bottle into the earth, my good President, and let the liquor he so loved weep for Sir John Autumnrod, gone to rest."

Grant nodded at her wisdom and poured out his heartbreak.

"Not iron, nor the Difference Engine"
by Kelly Fineman

Not iron, nor the Difference Engine
Of Babbage, shall outlive this powerful rhyme;
But you shall shine more bright in this paean
Than metal or machine worn down by time.
When wasteful war destroys device or steel,
And brawls lay waste to clockwork artistry,
Not Mars's sword nor war's relentless wheel
Will wipe this record of your memory.
'Gainst death and grinding gears of enmity
Shall you pace forth; your praise shall replicate
Itself in the eyes of all posterity
That wear this world out to the ending date.
Till judgment day when you yourself arise,
You live in this, and dwell in lover's eyes.

What You Fuel
by Jaymee Goh

"Good morrow, friends," Orsino's voice boomed as he entered the sitting room. The various courtiers murmured their greetings and bowed as he passed, a little leery of his girth and strength. Orsino's un-tuned body was strong unto itself, and he had tuned himself into a machine of strength, as demonstrated down at the mines that day. The drill-arm was now undone, replaced by a gripping hand.

Only Cesario did not move away. "My lord," came the soft, lilting voice that Orsino now found himself gratified to hear.

"Now, good Cesario," Orsino beckoned as he settled down into a cushioned chair. "That piece of song we heard last night—methought it did relieve my passion much, more than the whistles and music boxes of these brisk and metallic times. Let's hear but one verse tonight, shall we?"

"He's not here that should sing it, your lordship," Curio, one of the older retainers, interjected. He wasn't a smaller machine by any means, but still kept his distance.

"Who was it, then?"

"Feste the jester, my lord. An under-tuned fool that Lady Olivia's father took much delight in. He is about the house."

"I recall him now," Orsino replied. The under-tuned were not so rare, but often fell out of the notice of the mechanical nobility. Tuned, but not as extensively as they should be, they moved in between the un-tuned masses and the tuned masters, and were often sustained by talent and quick-thinking. "Seek him out, and play the song the while."

Curio bowed out quickly. After a moment or two while the courtiers glanced at each other to see who would wind the music-box, Cesario stepped out of line to tread on the key pedals that would wind up the mechanical orchestra in the corner. The others hoped he would break it, if only to demonstrate that their fears were well-founded.

Cesario, Orsino thought, was made of a high-grade steel, to not be intimidated by Orsino's own. "Thank you, boy," he sighed as the vibrations from the music began to wash over him. "If you shall ever love, remember me and my loyalty. How do you like this tune?"

Cesario smiled. "An echo to the very seat where Love is throned, my lord."

Orsino returned the smile. "A masterful response." He beckoned for Cesario to sit by him. "My life on't, but you know something of that which you speak, don't you, boy?"

A cough, and a blush coloured the flesh cheeks. "A little, by your favour."

When no other details were forthcoming, Orsino nudged the boy's foot. "Well, what kind of clockwork is she?"

"As like to your engines, sir." Cesario took a seat on the chair next to Orsino.

Orsino raised an eyebrow as he waved for a drink. "Oversized clockwork girls are good workers, but hardly a match for one of your shape. What years, i'faith?"

"About your years, sir."

"Too old, by heaven." Orsino shook his head, ready to dispense advice to his junior. "Let the woman key an elder than herself; so does her newer clockwork adapt more easily to him, and she remains a novelty in his affections. For, boy, however do we praise ourselves in the strength of our metals, our fancies are more giddy and unfirm, more longing, wavering, sooner lost and worn, than women's are."

Cesario only retained the smile. Of course Orsino could not know young, newly-tuned Cesario was really named Viola, that she was clockwork, which was why she always declined to refill her fuel with him; he could not see under her breastplate that her engine was complemented by a mainspring that she would gladly give him the key to wind. Instead, she merely said, "I think it well, my lord."

"Then let your love be younger than yourself, or your affection cannot last the pressure. For women make sweet music, but their song, once wound by keepers, lasts not very long."

Viola thought this over for a moment; being among the engine-bearing men had earned her many insights into the way they saw her clockwork sisters. "That may be so, though you may find: their song lasts long, so long their love they wind."

Orsino laughed, and Cesario smirked. Before the duke could rebut, the under-tuned motley came skipping in, Curio shaking his head at the informality behind the clown. Feste's helmet was several discarded plates clumsily welded together—cogs here and bolts piled high there, and a twig sticking out a pipe on top. Perhaps it was purposefully slipshod.

"Ah, fellow!" Orsino held out his hands in welcome. "Come, the song we had last night. Mark it, Cesario; it may be old and plain, sung by spinners and knitters and threaders in the textile depths, but it's the simple truth of innocent love. A fine song for one as yourself."

To Duke Orsino, perhaps the song was about heartbreak, but when the clown began singing, Viola heard a song about death and dying.

Orsino's finger tapped on the arm of his chair as he listened.

"... My part of death, no one so true, did share it..."

Viola's eyes flicked to Orsino's face then back at the clown. She could feel her heart slowing to match the tempo of the song. She didn't like the song, not because it was not beautiful, but because she was so close to tears as to reveal her true state.

"... Not a flower, not a flower sweet..."

—⚞—

Viola remembered too well the way the parachutes lay on the ground like lilies, her frantic shaking of the sailors' shoulders, only to discover her brother was simply not among them. She managed to keep calm to tend to their engines, oil necessary joints, and use her delicate fingers to clean internal pipes and crankshafts.

"What country, friend, is this?" she asked the captain, dodging the hiss of his ventilation pipe as she tightened a bolt on his shoulder.

"Illyria, my lady."

"Illyria. That was not our destination."

"No, lady."

"Didst you see my brother?" she asked softly, dreading the answer.

The captain's head swivelled around to face her. "Ah, lady, let me comfort you with chance. Assure yourself, after our ship did split, I saw him jump beside you, and his parachute opened fully before the updraft caught him and separated him from the rest of us. Perchance he survived, if it's any comfort."

She smiled, but only a little, and smartly rapped on his shoulderplate. "You're right—my own escape should give me hope for him." She found a pouch in a pocket. "For saying so, there's coal. Know'st thou this country?"

"Lady, I was born and tuned here, not three hours from this city."

"And who governs here?" Viola asked, getting to her feet and offering her hand to the captain.

Two sailors came to help lift the bulky captain to his feet, providing him balance as he checked the widgets on his sides. "A duke, Orsino by name."

"Orsino! My father spoke of him once. He was unkeyed then."

"Still is." The captain found his balance. "Until

recently. When I last passed through these parts, I heard gossip that he courts the fair Olivia."

"And what's she?" Viola scanned the distance, at the glow emanating from the city.

"Of the finest artisanal work, who lost her father and brother died within the last year. Out of love and loyalty to them, she refuses to give up her key to any man."

"I could go to her," Viola mused aloud, "and serve her, until a more appropriate time to reveal myself." It would be a good arrangement. Olivia was like herself: with no key-keeper, at risk of scandal. If Lady Olivia weathered the scandal, Viola would henceforth have an example. If not, she could have a confidante in someone who shared her secret shame.

"No, lady. She'll admit no kind of suit. Not even the Duke's."

Viola pursed her lips for a few moments, nonplussed; it was irregular to refuse the protection of powerful engines. "Then I'll serve this Duke," she said decisively. "Present me as a servant to him; it may be worth thy pains."

"Then my lady must conceal what she is, and I'll be your aid in any disguise as is your intent." The captain was clearly not going to argue. Viola had clashed enough times with men on the ship. "I know a tuner not far from here, to re-shape your form in whichsoever way you please."

Viola continued to stare into the distance, but she smiled at the suggestion. When she finally spoke, her voice was even and firm. "Then get me pistons, as like my brother's; though he be gone, he'll be in my mirrors."

—⚉—

"... Lay me, o where sad true lover never find my grave, to weep there.."

Sebastian never got a coffin, nor a grave. Viola swallowed and clapped her hands to hide her ticking as the song ended.

Orsino nodded avuncularly at Cesario's obvious pleasure in the song and threw a purse to the clown. "There's for your pains."

"No pains, sir." Feste bowed as he caught the purse, catching the twig before it fell out. "I take pleasure in singing, sir."

"I'll pay your pleasure, then."

"Truly, sir, and pleasure will be paid one time or another." Feste waggled his brows suggestively.

Orsino grinned. "Give me now leave to leave thee."

Another exaggerated bow. "And the melancholy god protect you, and the blacksmith make your shoulder plates of rainbow titanium, for your mind is very opal. I would have that men of such constancy be put to air, that their business might be every port, and their intent every cloud; for that's it that always makes a good voyage of nothing." The clown did several quick twirls on his heels, gracefully exiting. "Farewell!"

Cesario tried very hard not to giggle.

"Let all the rest give place." Orsino waved at the rest of the courtiers.

Everyone else hustled out, relieved and anxious at the same time. Cesario made a move to get up, but

Orsino held out a hand. The room grew quiet as the soft sounds of bodily engines receded.

Almost abruptly, Orsino turned to Cesario. "Once more, Cesario, get thee to yond same clockwork cruelty. Tell her my love, more noble than the world, prizes not quantity of dirty coal; tell her the mines that fortune hath bestowed upon her I hold indifferent as fortune, but 'tis that miracle that is her un-tuned beauty that attracts my soul."

With schooled features to not betray what was going on within, Viola remembered the first time Orsino requested this. It was not so long ago...

"Look you, sir. Is't not well done?" Olivia asked archly as she held up her veil. It was the first time Viola had ever seen such a beauty, and on an un-tuned face, too. It was also the first time she had ever met the Lady Olivia. However predisposed she had been to the lady until then, all goodwill vanished for a brief mad second as she considered that this was Orsino's love, and thus, Viola's rival, if Viola had been allowed to inhabit the facade called Cesario.

"Excellently done, if God did all," Viola bit out, and regretted the next moment how peevish she sounded. Who was she to question whether a woman's face was sculpted or un-tuned? Viola had been asked several times if her face was natural, and she knew how tiresome it was to have her face doubted.

"'Tis en-diamonded, sir; 'twill ensure wind and weather," Olivia replied in a brittle voice.

"A true blend of red and white that the skilful hand of that great artisan Nature e'er laid on," Viola offered with a bow. "Lady, you are the cruellest she alive if you will lead these graces to the grave, and leave no copy."

Lady Olivia laughed then. "O, sir, I will not be so hard-hearted. I will give out diverse blueprints of my beauty. It shall be inventoried, and every wire, spring, and article labelled to my will." She made a little gesture, as if writing down a list. "Item: two lips, indifferent red; item, two gray eyes, with lids to them; item, one neck, one chin, and so forth. Were you sent hither to catalogue me?"

Something in Viola started then; she found herself bristling at this clockwork-tuned woman who refused to acknowledge her engines as Cesario. All clockwork knew their inferiority to pistons. "I see you what you are; you are too proud; but even if you were a dismantler, you are fair." She was appalled at the words which stumbled forth. Men did call women dismantlers more often, and all tuned women considered it hurtful, as they were more easily taken apart. Her dismay at her gaffe must have shown, because Olivia's eyes were bright as they took in the unexpected sympathy across the young gentleman's face. Viola kneeled on one knee before Olivia, gazing up at her earnestly. "My lord and master loves you."

"Your lord does know my mind," Olivia replied softly. "I cannot love him. Yet I suppose him virtuous, know him noble, of great estate, of fresh and stainless steel; in voices well divulged, free, learned, and valiant, and in shape and nature a gracious person. Yet I cannot love him." She looked away, her eyes staring at something that wasn't there. "He might have took his answer long ago."

Viola could feel her gears clicking in curiosity. "If I did love you in my master's flame," she began carefully, "in your denial I would find no sense; I do not understand it."

Olivia turned back to Viola then, a sardonic smile on her lips. "Why, what would you?"

So much for drawing out the lady's reasons for not loving Orsino. She took back on the role of the wooing messenger. "Spin up a cumulus at your port and call upon my soul within the cloud," she began, gesturing as she spoke, "write loyal cantons of contemned love and sing them loud even in the dead of night; hallo your name to the emptiness of the skies and make the charged lightning in the air thunder: 'Olivia!'" She sprang into the air to show the expanse that would cry the lady's name. When she settled back down on her knees, she grinned up. "O, you would not rest between the elements of air and space, but you would pity me."

The answer was slow in coming, but satisfactory: the lady smiled with deep amusement. "You might do much." Then a surprising question. "What is your parentage?"

"Above my fortunes, yet my state is well. I have well-oiled pistons."

Lady Olivia nodded. "Get you to your lord. I cannot love him. Let him send no more." Viola frowned, and Olivia quickly added, "Unless, perchance, you come to me again to tell me how he takes it." She rose to her feet, and Viola rose with her. "Fare you well," she said gently, and took out a small purse from the folds of her dress. "I thank you for your pains. Spend this for me."

Viola frowned at the purse and stepped back. "I'm no lackey, lady, so keep your purse. It is my master who lacks recompense. May Love make the heart you shall love of flint, and your fervour, like my master's, be placed in contempt." She saluted Lady Olivia smartly. "Farewell, fair cruelty."

With that, Viola had stalked off, unhappy with the impossible situation she had been placed in. To speak with piston strength, she felt, was well; cursing her clockwork kin was twice the hell.

—⚉—

As Cesario, Viola stared at newly polished boots. "But if she cannot love you, sir?"

Orsino sat up in his chair at the answer. "I cannot be so answered."

"Sooth, but you must," Viola insisted. "Say that some lady, as perhaps there is, hath for your love as great a pang of heart as you have for Olivia. You cannot love her. You tell her so. Must she not then be answered?" It was the least she could do for Olivia, but as she watched Orsino's face flush with anger, she doubted her tactics.

"There's no women's gears can bide the grinding of so strong a passion as love doth give my heart," Orsino rose from his chair in agitation. He walked to the window, gesticulating as he spoke, "No woman's heart is so big as to hold much; they lack retention. Their love may be called reflection, not produced from the flesh, but the mainspring."

Viola felt both pistons and gears inside her grind faster and faster in her own increasing anger at Orsino's tirade.

"Make no compare between that love a woman can bear me and that I owe Olivia," he finished, now fully angry, and swung back at her, as if daring her to respond.

She took up the challenge. "Aye, but I know–"

"What dost thou know?"

"Too well what love women to men may owe," she snapped. "In faith, they are as true of heart as we."

The words hung in the air for several moments, Viola not quite believing she had said that, and to her superior, even. She had always wanted to hear a man say that, always wanted hear a man defend womanhood, since she could never say it herself. And now, with the pistons furiously pumping next to all her clockwork insides, she could say it, as a man, to another man. Incredible, how the presence of the piston engine counted her as his peer, even though she was half Orsino's size.

Orsino was scowling with all the scepticism typical of the men she knew, especially the tuned ones. She could hear his body hiss as it relieved the tension from his anger, and in the light of the sunset framing his body, saw the steam rise.

She remained still, her heart ticking away the seconds it took for him to stir from his position at the window and walk back to his chair. He leaned back to make himself comfortable, and his posture reminded Viola of the first time she walked around with her new engines. What a remarkable difference they made!

With this kind of physique, no wonder tuned men took up space the way they did.

"My father had a daughter who loved a man as perhaps I might have your lordship, were I a woman," she offered, then cleared her throat as he turned to regard her quizzically. She felt her cheek flush with the inadvertent confession.

"What's her story?" Orsino asked, a sardonic smile now playing at his lips. His eyes swept over her small frame, as if assessing where her keyhole might be, if she had been clockwork. Their eyes met, and for a moment she felt as though he knew she was clockwork.

"A blank, my lord," she said quickly to cover up the tick-tick-tick inside her. Doubtless, he considered her queer enough; Cesario was small, yet didn't mimic older courtiers the way newly-tuned youth normally did. He didn't need to know how mixed inside she was, in feeling or tuning. "She never told her love, but let concealment spread like rust under her porcelain cheeks. She pined in thought, and with her heart wound down in melancholy, sat like Patience on a monument." She stopped, and thought about the image. Was she really? She felt selfish, pathetic, piteous. "And smiled at her grief." And she smiled herself, hoping Orsino would see the tragedy on her Cesario's face. "Is this not love, indeed? Men may say more, swear more, but their shows are more than will."

"But did she die of her love, boy?" Orsino asked, the scepticism on his face easing.

Viola nearly bit her tongue. *I'm alive. I'm here. And I love you*, she thought, but instead said aloud, "I'm all the daughters of my father's house, and all his sons too, perhaps..." It was an honest answer. She was still clockwork Viola, but her pistons echoed her brother Sebastian.

Orsino nodded. "I am sorry for what I have asked you to remember," he grunted.

Viola swallowed uneasily, feeling her heart skip a tick at his sympathy. "Shall I to the lady, sir?" she asked.

"That's the theme." Orsino gestured to the table, at a jewellery case laying on it. "Go to her, tell her this: my love can give no place."

Viola took it, resisting the urge to peep into it. He held out his metal hand, and she walked over to kiss it. As she bent over, he used his un-tuned arm to ruffle her hair. There was a kindly smile on his face, which she was certain she had never seen when other courtiers were present.

Later in her room, she wound herself up carefully, and took a deep breath as she felt her mainspring tense up comfortably again. Then she splashed oil onto the joints and placed a handful of coal into the small firebox a little under her diaphragm. She contemplated her compact engine for a moment, and was pleased at how well her clockwork worked with it–it had been engineering of her own devising. Even the captain and the tuner had been impressed.

Yet... yet this self-same engine that made her a peer among pistons made her clockwork womanhood invisible to Orsino. "Who could know what I might have been, had my true form be freely seen?" she whispered to herself, listening to the light voice so often confused for a boy's. "I'm equal, 'tis true, but this ease is strife; whoe'er I woo, myself would be his wife."

"To me, fair friend, you never can be old"
by Tucker Cummings

To me, fair friend, you never can be old,
You are to me as you have always been.
Creator, yes, but handsome to behold
My clockwork heart still yearns for your aged skin.
'Twas forty years ago when you did grasp
My final flywheel, stirring me to life.
The perfumes of April scented that gasp
And turned me all at once into your wife.
My eyes on thee see only deeds and heart.
Thy beauty marches like a dial-hand,
My clockbound mind likewise declines with age,
My heart, for thee, ticks on by your command.
And if you should pass before my gears fail?
I'll follow thee beyond, where death's ships sail.

A Midsummer's Night Steam
by Scott Farrell

Down the airship's boarding ramp, Captain Titania's boots thumped with a strong, purposeful tempo. As one of the few female pilots in all of Atlantis, she didn't glide like a lazy cloudliner, buoyed by a balloon of super-light gas before the zephyr's gentle nudge. When flying through the night sky, her lunathopter required constant monitoring of attitude and velocity; that was precisely how Titania conducted herself as well.

Even in haste, however, Titania moved with the proud, stiff bearing of an officer steeled by experience in the Atlantean Air Armada. Her coal-black hair, cut primly short at the line of her jaw, bobbed briskly with each step. Protocols and formalities were never neglected in her presence, not even on a routine conveyance of post and passengers, which was why Titania's crew called her the "queen of the sky"–at least when they believed she was out of earshot.

Oversights and delays were unacceptable among her crew, and that made her current exit from the confines of the ship particularly troubling indeed.

Titania found her first officer and chief engineer both hunched beneath one of the ship's forward access cowlings, which was propped up to reveal the maintenance crawlway behind. A pressure-gas lamp hissed within the workspace, burning with a haze of cool blue light that mimicked the full moon's bright glow.

"Please you, Mr. Oberon," the captain said. "Explain why my lunathopter is on the ground instead of dancing the whistling winds and riding the gusts of the middle summer's spring, as it should be." She spoke in the nearly poetic diction of Atlantean High Dialect, the standard tongue aboard all working vessels of the empire, military and merchant alike. But tonight her formal, well-chosen words were underpinned with a distinct tone of anxiety.

A tall man with auburn locks and cheeks browned by the sun crawled from beneath the upraised panel. Rising to his feet, Oberon wiped the grease from his hands and gave the captain a quick salute. "Our battery banks are completely drained, captain," he explained. "And since we've nothing but our solar array to provide a supplemental charge, that news is ill-met by moonlight."

"We should have reached Atlantis with power to spare," Titania said. "I like not making emergency landings, especially near so populated a place as Athens. What's happened to the power? Have the mechanicals failed in their tasks?"

"The mechanical crew's not to blame, captain," announced another voice in a spirited, almost merry way from within the cramped work area. "You know

I'd've kept this filly foal in the sky, even if I had nothing but a dandelion seed and two dragonfly wings to hold her up. Ow!" The statement was punctuated by the sound of the speaker's head colliding with something metallic.

Though Titania bristled at the silly exaggeration, she had no qualms about her chief engineer's admirable skill with the complex system of chemical batteries, heating coils, and steam pistons that drove the ship's bank of impellers and stabilizers. Despite his physical challenges, Robin had kept the lunathopter flying on many occasions when, by all rights, it should have plunged to its destruction.

"Then what, say swiftly, has marooned us here?" the captain asked. "We tarry on this foreign soil upon peril of harsh penalty and loss of rank. The Athenian mere'atals are well known for their troublesome curiosity."

"*Mere'atal* is a term from an age of contemptuous discrimination, captain," Oberon said with a sharpness just short of insubordination. "Let us not refer to the people of Athens as 'merely human, if at all' to mock their want of sophisticated technology. I would not have you use such words before the crew, lest they believe you guilty of an unseemly prejudice... an erroneous belief, I'm sure, ma'am." His dutiful nod maintained the captain's dignity.

"Mistake not impatience for bias," Titania retorted. "For the protection of primitive peoples I have gone to no small efforts, so set your heart at rest and disclose our predicament."

With a clank and a whir, the chief engineer's oily

face appeared from under the cowling. Unlike the first officer, Robin couldn't lightly scoot himself from the maintenance crawlway. He sat in a chair fixed atop a compact springwork mechanism that turned a powerful rotor blade and lifted the device on a cushion of air. His legs were malformed and immobile; the mechanical chair allowed him freedom of movement. Over open ground, he could match the speed of a galloping horse.

"Locating the problem isn't the problem, captain," Robin said in answer to the captain. "Here's the roasted crab in the wassail bowl, right here."

Robin steered his hovering chair toward the captain and held up a harness of charred wiring. "Crisped in that thunderstorm we passed through this morning," he explained. "Shorted out the system, and since then we've been leaking power like a gossip spilling secrets in an alehouse."

"We've important passengers who expect to be in Atlantis on schedule," Titania said. "And they've paid richly for that passage. Can this be mended, then?"

"Mending's easy," Robin answered with a nod toward the ship. "I've got our junior mechanical in there now, and a good thing that boy's not grown much bigger'n an acorn cup, else we'd have no one who could wriggle in to make repair. We'll have those cables replaced before you can say Philomel, captain. Still, that's only half the fix."

"Like an empty goblet, the charge of our battery bank must be replenished," Oberon added. "We'll need several hours of sunlight before we're able to take the sky once more."

Titania inspected the ruined wiring. "My good Mr.

Robin, tell me: How much battery power need we to reach Atlantis?"

His hovering chair stabilized itself when he snapped his fingers. "Some small charge would do the trick," he said. "A bit more than a sneeze, and less than a swear, as they say."

"A pretty riddle," the captain said. "But we need a solution that's more than moonshine and dewdrops, Robin." Over the burned wires she looked at the two men. "Can we use the pneumathal?"

Oberon responded instantly: "That barbaric instrument? Use of those devices was abandoned years ago."

"Abandoned," Titania noted. "But never outlawed."

Oberon bristled. "What the law does not curtail, sheer decency may yet avoid." The pneumathal was a sort of distillation chamber, but instead of draining liquid or vapor, the device drew upon the *psychi*, the vital force of a human spirit, converting it into pure energy. The process wasn't lethal, but it always exacted a physical toll from its victim. "Who would you sacrifice to this life-thief?" Oberon demanded. "One of the men or women of the crew who's given you their allegiance? No ship of war is this, Titania, and regulations forbid requiring any Atlantean subject to undergo torture or ordeal as part of their contracted service."

Ignoring his caustic tone, the captain said, "I do not propose we use it on one of our own." She nodded toward the raised shroud, where the sounds of repairs were coming from within. "But our junior mechanical, as I know, is not born of Atlantean blood. He is an Indian child whose mother was killed by unfortunate accident with a trading craft. He was taken in and nurtured as a fosterling at one of our distant colonies. It was from there that he was given to us as a young squire, to rear up as a member of our crew."

"Does that lower him to the status a piece of machinery to be dismantled at your command?" Oberon asked. "Or a beast of burden to be whipped for your conveyance? Because he was not Atlantis-born, is he only a... mere'atal?"

"No," she answered. "But he is less guarded by the protections of the Great Atlantean Charter. And unlike a machine or any laboring beast, I will see him justly rewarded for this sacrifice. When we return to Atlantis, he will be accorded standing as a true subject of the realm. I will take him as a ward of my family, and raise him as I would my own son."

"With respect, captain, thou speakest awrong," Robin interjected, his voice suddenly devoid of its usual cheer. "I would not put that boy through the suffering I've known. This is the devil's bargain of old."

Titania replied, "It is a bargain that, in the times of our fathers, gave you this Powered Unidirectional Clockwork Kopter you sit upon. And by its providence, you were granted admittance to the Atlantean Academy and trained as a mechanical. Wanting these advantages, your life might have been spent toiling in the mines of Lemuria, or auctioned at the Illyrian slave markets. And such a life is short and savage indeed."

"An' I would willingly give up my mechanical chair and my education too, and submit to a miner's toil or slave's servitude, if only to set my own feet upon the ground and walk," Robin said. "I had not that choice when I was but a babe."

"Many families such as yours were raised from poverty by these terms," Titania said. "There is no time to brook debate. Expediency and regulation both lend me their weight." The captain's tone signaled that further dissention would not be taken lightly. "Robin, fetch the boy."

Robin drew a measured breath, then obediently steered his chair back to the crawlway. "Lad," he called sharply. "Finish with that and stand forth."

Oberon knew he risked the captain's wrath by pressing on, but his position and rank afforded him liberties that Robin lacked. Quietly, he said, "Spare the boy and surely by morning's light, we can employ our solar array to gather up the sun's radiant potency. It will not take so long that we will be discovered by the Athenians. There is no need for this dreadful urgency."

"There is more need than you now know," Titania whispered as she checked to see that Robin was still distracted. "I have communication from Atlantis this very night summoning us to port with all haste, for in our capital city, a contagious fog has been sucked up from the sea, which, falling on the land, afflicts our people with a plague of rheumatic diseases. One of our passengers is an apothecary from an Oriental colony, who bears with him medicines to cure this sickening air before it overbears the city walls. To guard 'gainst panic, the crew knows not of this, but with every passing hour the situation worsens. If we delay past morning, we will surely come too late."

Hearing this, Oberon's face became grim. "These are unkind tidings."

"Cruel circumstances demand cruel decisions," the captain concurred. "We must be gone ere sunup, or all Atlantis stands in hazard." Seeing Oberon's nod of concession, she said, "Tonight the lives of thousands may be saved by the inconvenience of one."

Oberon pondered Titania's statement, then said, "Perhaps there is another recourse. The pnementhal may draw power from any source which is remarkable in its purity. I know of a resinite, an herbaceous exudant found in these woods like unto a morsel of bright gold, that contains an energy so potent it can be tapped to create a shocking force. Among the people of the East it is sometime called *ambar*, though the superstitious Athenians wear it as a charm and name it *ilektronika* in honor of their sun god."

"I have heard tell of it," Titania said. "But rare it is, and hard to find."

"Grant me leave to use the Aero-Sonic Sensor to discover a cache of this resinite," Oberon said. "We will use the pneumathal to draw its power and avoid doing harm to this Indian child placed in your trust."

Titania thought on Oberon's suggestion as she watched the boy emerge from the battery compartment's narrow crawlway. He stood beside Robin's chair, his simple tunic frayed and mottled with dark stains of rust and grease. His limbs were slender with the quick growth of youth. She guessed the boy couldn't have seen more than ten summers, and he would grow broad-shouldered and strong in time, if given the opportunity.

"You called for me, m'lady?" the boy asked shyly.

"Come with me, lad," she said. As she guided

the boy out of the lamplight and toward the boarding ramp, she looked over her shoulder and added, "Use the sensor cowl, Mr. Oberon. Mind you, dawn is near. Bring me this extraordinary herbal resinite ere then and we will employ it to give juice to our ship. But come the sunrise, I will use that pneumathal to get us to Atlantis, one way or another. Until then, I will not part with this boy."

"Hobs and goblins," Robin exclaimed in wonder as he watched Titania depart with the boy at her side. "The captain's letting one of the crew set foot in her own compartment? And a mere'atal, no less! I'd venture our young mechanical is in for a night he won't soon forget."

Oberon nodded. "We must do our best to get that little changeling boy from her. He may be but a henchman of our crew, but he does not deserve this injury." Wiping his hands once more on the oily rag tucked through his belt, he said, "Let's to it, then. We've much to do; there is no time for idleness."

A little company of amateur actors had gathered near the great Duke's Oak, a mile outside the walls of Athens. They met by the dim glow of a single candle lamp. They had come to the secluded woods to rehearse a play they would perform in honor of the duke himself. One rehearsal, they felt, would be plenty of practice for such an auspicious occasion.

Waving his hands with frantic impatience, the director, Peter Quince, signaled for quiet. With the players' attention on him, Quince tittered, "Here's a marvelous convenient place for our rehearsal. This green plot shall be our stage, this hawthorn brake our tiring-house; and we will do it in action as we will do it before the duke."

One tall fellow stood a pace apart from the others of the troupe. With a snort of pique, he said, "Peter Quince!"

"What sayest thou, bully Bottom?"

"There are things in this comedy of Pyramus and Thisby that will never please. First, Pyramus must draw a sword to kill himself; which the ladies cannot abide. How answer you that?"

Nodding, Tom Snout the tinker said, "By'r lakin, a parlous fear," and beside him, the tailor called Starveling suggested, "I believe we must leave the killing out, when all is done."

Alarmed at the suggestion of reducing his own part in the play, Bottom held up a hand. "Not a whit," he said. "I have a device to make all well. Write me a prologue," he said to Peter Quince, "and let the prologue seem to say, we will do no harm with our swords, and that Pyramus is not killed indeed. And, for the more better assurance, tell them that Pyramus is not a brigand, but a soldier gallant, who is newly turned from the Trojan War. For how else should Thisby fall in love with him but he has fought with disclusion? And so the audience should know this, let Pyramus wear gilt armor and a crested helmet atop his head so the ladies will see of his valor."

Peter Quince spoke through clenched teeth. "Well, we will have such a prologue, and it shall be written in eight and six. But Master Bottom, as to the other, there is no armor, and we have no crested helmet unless you would wear one of Tom Snout's tin kettles upon your head."

"That would be most rare!" the tinker commented with a giggle.

"Let us hear no more of armor and helmets, Bottom," Peter Quince demanded. "Come, sit down, every mother's son, and rehearse your parts. Pyramus, you begin. When you have spoken your speech, enter into that brake, and so every one according to his cue!"

The actors stepped away from the glow of Peter Quince's candle and took their places deep in the shadows. Bottom assumed a pose at center stage and began his line, "Thisby, the flowers of odious savours sweet…"

But Bottom's attention was not on his words, which Peter Quince pointed out with his correction: "Odours, odours." Bottom was hardly listening, though. He finished his line woodenly and made his exit from the stage, but he was still imagining Pyramus as a gallant Trojan war hero. He could just envision how splendid he would look, appearing before the ladies of Athens with a plumed helmet of gold upon his head.

—ᴡ—

Five hundred paces from the lunathopter, Oberon and Robin stood by a stream near a grove of tall ferns. The metrical ticking of the springworks that powered Robin's hovering chair was nearly lost beneath the sound of running water.

"At this distance, the ship will not affect our readings," the first officer said as he put down his satchel. "Robin, give me the Aero-Sonic Sensor cowl. Let us see if it may discern the presence of the ambar exudant nearby."

"I've dialed its most delicate setting," Robin told him. "It will detect a maiden's lovesick sigh amidst a stormy gale."

"I pray this time you do not exaggerate," Oberon replied.

Carefully, Robin handed Oberon the device. Built to allow a scouting party to search for trace amounts of valuable natural resources, the sensory cowl was an assortment of instruments attached to a sturdy leather headpiece. Tinted goggles with a selection of lenses could enhance or mask varying hues of light. A pair of polished bronze cups on top created a sonic relay that, via echoing squeaks and chirps, was capable of determining the density and composition of faraway objects with great precision.

Most useful of all, however, was the filter snout that protruded below the goggles. It employed an intricate system of bellows to gather and analyze air samples, detecting minute particles borne on the breeze.

The array was powered by its own battery pack, suspended from the back of the unit by a harness of thick, twisting cables. Oberon placed the device atop his head, activated the bellows, and adjusted the goggles to augment the pale illumination of the moonlight.

"See you anything?" Robin asked as the air system began its rhythmic huffing and wheezing.

Scanning the landscape, Oberon watched the

tiny dials within the helmet closely. Finally, one of the needles twitched and Oberon focused the sonic probes on a single spot.

"'Tis there," he said softly, making incremental adjustments to the detectors. "On a bank where wild thyme blows, where oxlips and nodding violet grows, quite over-canopied with luscious woodbine, with sweet musk-roses and with eglantine."

"I never realized you were such a botanist, sir," Robin commented.

"Not botany," Oberon said. "Navigation. I don't want you to lose your way."

"Me?" Robin wondered.

Oberon explained, "That bank is a league or more distant. I'll never reach it on foot. But along these wooded paths, your chair will give you great speed. Fetch me this herbaceous resin; and be thou here again ere the leviathan can swim a league."

Robin smiled as he gave the springwork mechanism a crank, happy to be of more use than greasing gears and connecting steam conduits. "You can count on me, Mr. O. I'll put a girdle round about the earth in forty minutes!"

Oberon laid a steadying hand on Robin's shoulder. "You needn't compass the world on your powered sled, Robin. Just fetch our juice and be thou here again."

Robin was reaching for the lever that regulated his propulsion fans when Oberon stopped him. "Hold. The sensor is picking up something more." He adjusted the frequency of the sonic detectors. "Athenian voices I hear, loitering near your destination."

"Even by darkness, and with my chair to speed me,

I dare not approach these primitives."

"I came aready for just such a complication," Oberon said. He removed the bulky sensor helmet and placed it on the ground, then opened his satchel and brought out a long garment. Its dark fabric was the same filmy material that coated the exterior of the lunathopter. When electrified, the fabric took on the aspect of a moonbeam or a thread of mist in the darkness, thereby concealing whatever it encompassed.

"This aoratosmantle is fully charged," Oberon said, the cloak flashing like a dark mirror in his grasp.

Robin took the cloak, drew it around his shoulders, and found the sensitive contact strip on the garment's front. Like other Atlantean devices made to confound human senses, when activated, the cloak had a disorienting effect more powerful than a draught of strongest ale. "Guard your sight," Robin warned as he connected two hair-thin copper wires along the cloak's edges. With a flash of deep violet light, the place where Robin's chair hovered suddenly appeared empty of all but soft grass, fern leaves, and moon shine.

"I'll be back with your resin-stones ere you can whistle a roundel, sir," said Robin's disembodied voice. The turmoil of air from the sled's rotor was the only indication of his departure.

Oberon shut the satchel, shouldered it, and returned to the lunathopter. His mind was already tabulating the speed and vector of their homeward journey, as well as the amount of battery power the ship would need to draw through the pneumathal to reach the shores of Atlantis.

Preoccupied with these details, Oberon left the

sensory cowl behind him, hidden under the sprawling leaves of a fern.

—⚍—

Behind the Duke's Oak, Bottom paced anxiously, waiting for Frances Flute to speak the line that was his signal to return to the candlelit rehearsal space. In the darkness, he had to step carefully to keep from stubbing his toes on roots and stones hidden by the underbrush. "Frances Flute must say, 'As true as truest horse that yet would never tire...' and then I must speak my next line in a matrimonious voice. Now, to observe the sound of my cue."

But crickets chirping and the rushing of a nearby stream were the only noises Bottom heard, and he was certain those were not his cues.

Waist-deep in a patch of ferns, Bottom began to worry that he'd strayed too far from the tree to hear Flute's voice. Now, in the deep shadows, he wasn't even certain which way he'd come. He'd lost the glow of Peter Quince's candle, and all the trees looked the same in the moonlight. Standing tip-toe, he called tentatively, "Frances Flute? Peter Quince? Lads? Are you ready for my appearance? Ah... hello, what is here?"

Curious, he reached down and found a strange object lying near his foot.

"This is fortunistic," he said gladly as he raised the odd thing into the moonlight. "Now Pyramus shall appear refutably heroic before the ladies!"

Straightening his posture proudly, Bottom held the battery cables aside and placed the Aero-Sonic Sensor on his head.

"A gallant helmet," he said as the sonic cups twirled. "A triumvirate helmet whose plumes ride upon the breeze!"

Settling the device on his brow comfortably, Bottom's thumb inadvertently spun a control dial, replacing the goggles' starlight lenses with a darkened set meant to dim the noonday sun. Believing his sudden blindness was caused by a crooked fit of his helmet, Bottom continued to twist and prod until he poked the air analyzer's control switch.

Whreee, groaned the bellows as they drew in a sample; then *vhaaaw* as the air cycled back out through the cowl's sensitive filters.

With the cowl covering his ears, Bottom mistook the puffing noises for his companions' voices in the distance. "Aye! Where are my fellows? Where are my souls?" He pushed aside the branches as he tried to follow the sound. "Let me hear my – *wheee* – cue, and I will – *haawwh* – answer!"

―⚊―

In the calm environs of her small stateroom, Titania pondered her earlier dispute with Oberon. He was an admirable officer, but his compassion for mere'atals like this boy was sometimes maddening.

The true superiority of the Atlantean spirit was the basis on which the Great Charter had been established. Only after rigorous toil or physical hardship could men of simple comprehension be allowed to join the population of Atlantis–without making appropriate sacrifice, primitive peoples could never grasp the import of Atlantis's magnificent culture and technological achievement. That was why the primitives had to be protected against knowledge of the civilization of Atlantis, and why Atlanteans traveling among the primitives were required to obscure their presence.

The captain rubbed at her weary, burning eyes, then read the latest bulletin once more. *Return to port with all possible speed*, it said. *Conditions worsening; all previous orders and assignments declared void; any personnel causing delays in delivery of medicinal supplies will be subject to severest penalties.*

Titania hadn't slept in more than twenty-four hours, and it had been almost that long since she'd had a meal. Fatigue dulled her troubled mind.

Across the polished chart table, she watched the Indian boy paging slowly through her navigational compendium. It was the nearest thing she had to a picture book to entertain the child; he seemed content to pore over the sketches of shorelines and mountain ranges.

Does he conceive the wonders laid out upon those pages? Or, like an insect crawling on the skin of an airship, is the enormity of what he sees beyond him?

The sudden rattle of the ship's intercom disrupted her thoughts. Titania brushed her hair back, lifted the gleaming brass earpiece from its cradle and said, "This is the captain."

"Mr. Tseid here, ma'am," said the voice on the other end.

"What is it, Mr. Tseid?"

"Well, it's the passengers, ma'am," the junior purser

said. "The apothecary. He's down here in the lounge with his two assistants, and he demands to know why we've stopped. He seems to think there's some kind of crisis in Atlantis, ma'am."

Titania's jaw tightened. That was supposed to be guarded information. "Confine the good apothecary and his apprentices to the drawing area," she said. "I'll be right there."

Titania heard the worry in Tseid's voice as he responded, "Aye, aye, captain." She set down the earpiece sharply.

"Boy, I must needs go out," Titania said. "I'll be back soon. Stay here, and be content to look at the drawings. All right?"

"I thank you for letting me take my ease here, ma'am," the boy said politely. "I always learn much from texts such as these." He glanced back down to the map. "I hope someday to go to the Academy to learn more. To become a man of worth, like Robin. Or perhaps even a captain myself. Do you think I might pilot a ship like this one someday, ma'am?"

With a shrug, Titania replied, "You seem a bright lad." She met his eyes for a moment longer, then turned and left the stateroom without another word.

—⚏—

"Must I speak now?" Frances Flute asked timidly.

"Aye, marry, must you," Peter Quince explained as he waved a copy of the script before Flute's face. Quince pointed in the direction of Bottom's recent exit and said, "For you must understand he goes to see a noise that he heard, and is to come again."

Flute cleared his throat and squinted at the script. "Most radiant Pyramus," he squeaked in falsetto, "most lily-white of hue, of color like the red rose on the triumphant brier, most briskly juvenal and eke most lovely Jew, as true as truest horse that yet would never tire, I'll meet thee, Pyramus, at Ninny's tomb."

Peter Quince rolled his eyes heavenward. "'Ninus' tomb, man,' he corrected. "Why, you must not speak that yet! That you answer to Pyramus." He shook his head wearily. "You speak all your part at once, cues and all! Pyramus, enter! Your cue is past. It is 'never tire.'"

But Bottom did not reenter. The shadowed forest lawn fell still and silent.

"Oh! As true as truest horse!" Flute repeated more loudly. "That yet would never tire!"

Then a silhouette appeared through the thick branches of the Duke's Oak. At first, the players thought their eyes were deceived by the some trick of the shadows. But when he stepped into the candlelight, the troupe beheld a very different Bottom than the one who'd recently made his exit.

Bottom bellowed: "If I were fair, Thisby, I were only thine…"As he orated, his voice boomed and rumbled through the massive contraption on his head. His friends could see little but the bizarre outline of the device, and its size and configuration baffled them all.

"B-b-b-Bottom!" Tom Snout stammered. "Thou art changed. What do I see on thee?"

Bottom glanced from side to side, searching for the person who was speaking. The sonic relay cups buzzed and chirped as they tried to determine the composition of trees, players, candle, and everything else in the vicinity. As Bottom leaned forward to peer through the darkened lenses, Snout and the others saw the glow of the interior dials and gauges reflected from within.

"What do you see?" Bottom roared. "You see an ass head – *Wheee!*– of your own, do you? *Hawww!*"

"Bless thee, Bottom!" Peter Quince squealed. "Bless thee! Thou art translated!"

The director dashed away into the woods with his players hot on his heels. A moment later there was nothing left to mark their evacuation but a scatter of discarded scripts in the weeds.

Realizing he'd been abandoned, Bottom snorted. "I see their knavery. This is to make an ass of me. To fright me, if they could. But I will not stir from this place!– *heee!*– Do what they can! I will walk up and down here, and they shall hear that I –*haww!*– am not afraid."

Blinded by the goggles and distracted by the whirling dials and buzzing sonic relay, Bottom strode away into the trees, trying desperately to maintain a dignified posture.

"And I will not take off my plumed helmet," he said over the bellows' noise. "No matter how much they try to make an ass of me."

—⚄—

Robin checked the linear calculator, which indicated he'd steered his chair more than a league through the moonlit woods. This was where Oberon said he'd find the deposit of crystallized resin. He carefully removed the aoratosmantle and leaned forward precariously to search beneath a thick tangle of foliage. He was beginning to doubt Oberon's readings when his fingers touched something hard. Carefully, he brought it out of the shadows.

"Night and silence," he exclaimed softly. "What is here?" It was a nugget of ambar nearly as large as a man's fist. With a satisfied nod, Robin turned to drop it into a pouch hanging behind his seat.

Before he could resettle himself for the return journey, however, a pair of aggravated voices shattered the quiet.

"Relent, Lysander," said one. "And in sweet Hermia's love, yield thy crazed title to my certain right!"

"You have her father's love, Demetrius," replied the other. "Let me have Hermia's. Do you marry him!"

The voices approached quickly, each man's tone growing sharper and angrier with every proclamation of love the other made. Hearing this, Robin struggled to replace the aoratosmantle. He barely had it over his shoulders when a nearby branch snapped and two men came into view, each dressed for traveling with breeches and heavy sandals, satchels on their shoulders, and swords at their sides to ward against thieves on the roadway.

With not an instant to spare, Robin yanked the cloak into place and engaged its seal. With a flash, the aoratosmantle shrouded Robin from the sight of the arguing men. He reached for the operating lever and set off toward the lunathopter at full speed, scattering oxslip petals and violet blossoms behind him.

The two men fell speechless, their minds dazzled by

the cloak's effect. Rancor had been replaced by sudden delirium and giddiness. Demetrius smiled and giggled at the glow of the moon, the cushion of grass under his feet, the scent of nighttime flowers. Everything was more vivid and delightful than it had been just a moment ago. As his laughter abated, he said, "Peace, Lysander, peace. This western wind cools my heated blood. Let us be friends and quarrel no more over Hermia and Helena."

Lysander's mind was fogged with a similar sense of rapture. He scarcely remembered what he'd been saying a moment earlier–something about "love" and "a doting woman." He hardly heard a word Demetrius said; only the last one caught his attention. "Helena? Transparent Helena?" he muttered in confusion, "Nature shows art, that through her bosom makes me see her heart."

Lysander then looked to his rival and said, "You are unkind, Demetrius. Be not so. For you love Hermia, this you know I know." He shook his head to bring his scattered thoughts into focus. "And here, with all good will, with all my heart, in Hermia's love I yield you up my part. And yours of Helena to me bequeath, whom I do love and will do till my death."

"Let her alone. Speak not of Helena. Take not her part," Demetrius warned as his fingers touched the hilt of the sword at his side. "For if thou dost intend never so little show of love to her, thou shall aby it."

Lysander spat contemptuously as his own hand lighted upon his weapon. One swift move brought the blade out to glitter in the moonlight. "Now follow, if thou darest," he threatened. "To try whose right, of mine or thine, is most in Helena."

Demetrius eagerly drew in reply. "Follow!" he snarled as his anger rose to a fury. "Nay, I'll go with thee, cheek by jole!" In the next moment, the woods rang with the brazen clash of swords.

—ɷ—

In the ship's passenger lounge, Titania arrived to find the apothecary upbraiding her crew. "I demand you get this lunathopter underway at once. We will be beyond our scheduled arrival in Atlantis. If we longer delay, I will report this unapproved postponement to your superior officers." He brushed fastidiously at the lapels of his long coat to demonstrate his displeasure.

Titania approached the gathering and motioned the crew to give her room. "Master chemist," she soothed. "Our progress waits upon a small mechanical difficulty. We will shortly be embarked towards our port once more."

"Let it be so," the apothecary said. "Our mission requires much haste. But who comes here?"

Titania glanced stiffly over her shoulder. For a moment, she wondered why Oberon had come to the passengers' area wearing the Aero-Sonic Sensor he'd taken from the equipment storage compartment.

But an instant later, she realized this was not her first officer; not unless he'd exchanged his uniform for the simple garb of one of the local primitives.

This was an Athenian.

Struggling to sound calm, Titania said, "Mr. Tseid, escort our guests to their cabins and fetch them some refreshment from the galley." Turning back to the apothecary, she added, "You have my assurance, sir, that we will…"

"Coddle me not like some wealthy pilgrim or tender newlywed," he scolded. "I will observe your preparations for departure here, and make full report to the Atlantean governance council upon our return."

With a forced smile, Titania motioned the man to take his ease in one of the stuffed armchairs provided for passenger comfort. But comfortable wasn't what she wanted him to be; she wanted him back in the seclusion of his quarters.

The apothecary could cite Atlantean ordinances by chapter and verse, and he was an ardent proponent of the law's strictures against contact with primitive peoples. Allowing one of them to wander onboard a ship–in possession of a sensitive piece of scientific equipment, no less–was a violation of practically every provision of the Great Charter.

If the apothecary reported this, Titania knew she would never fly again.

With a curt nod to the junior officer, Titania whispered, "Mr. Tseid! Devise a distraction until I can get this Athenian off the ship."

Mr. Tseid's eyes widened. "Yes, ma'am," he answered quickly as he, too, realized that the man wearing the sensory cowl was not Oberon.

Mr. Tseid struck up a conversation with the apothecary as the captain approached their uninvited guest. "Whither wander thou, traveler?" she asked in her calmest tone.

"Traveler am I none, good dame," Bottom said.

"My fellows have pulled a jest on me and run for home, leaving me here in the dark. But I might prove that I have more wit than the lot of them if I follow this path out of the woods and back to Athens."

Nearing him, Titania noted that the cowl's goggles were obscured by the smoked lenses. Even in the ship's bright gaslamps, the man could hardly see beyond the distance of his arm. No wonder he thought himself in a darkened wood.

At last, thought the captain, a spin of fortune's wheel that may turn in our favor!

"Out of this wood do not desire to go," she said softly. "Thou shalt remain here whether thou will, or no."

Taking his arm with all the formality of an Atlantean dignitary, Titania gracefully turned the interloper away from the seating area and back toward the doorway.

"Methinks, mistress, that you have uncommon good wits," Bottom said over the chuffing of the bellows. "What sort of place is this, lady? A tented garden, or some private bower where we may take our ease?"

"No, wanderer," Titania explained. "It is a ship, and thou must depart from hence ere it sails from port."

Bottom gasped in time with the air intake valve. "A ship, you say? What manner of vessel?"

"A ferry, sir," Titania explained. "And one that conveys passengers who must not be disturbed."

"Fairy," Bottom echoed. "Then you must be the fairy folk I've heard spoken of."

"Yes," Titania agreed. Noticing the unmistakable tone of fascination in the man's voice, she led him on. "And if thou walk with me, thou wilt be one of the ferry's spirits too."

"To dally in thy company, lady, would be a pleasure most deplorable!" Bottom replied. "But this plumed helmet grows wearious. Let me set it off."

"No, sweet lord," Titania said quickly. "For thy... helmet becomes thee well. Wear it and let me admire thy beauty."

Arm-in-arm, Titania escorted Bottom out of the lounge as a group of junior officers appeared from the galley, hastily serving drinks to the passengers. Obliviously, Bottom spoke on, describing the helmets worn by several mythic heroes, each of whom he expected Peter Quince to immortalize in verse. Titania nodded agreeably as she guided him along the main hall, and at last down the lunathopter's long boarding ramp.

When the two reached the bottom, the sonic relays atop the sensor cowl began swirling and vibrating as they probed the open night air.

"Forgive me, dear lady," Bottom said with a giggle. "But I feel an exposition of tickling come upon me. My skin is tender, and if my hair do but tickle me, I must scratch."

Before he could take off the cowl, the captain said, "There is no need for that. I'll give thee... ferry folk to attend on thee. Cobwebb! Mr. Tseid!"

A small gang of crewmen stood in their wake, gawking at the queen of the sky strolling along like a lovestruck maiden. Two of them dashed down the ramp at Titania's summons. "Ready!" one answered smartly, as the other piped up, "Aye!"

Taking Bottom's hands in her own, Titania sighed.

"Ferrymen, be kind and courteous to this gentleman. Hop in his walks and gambol in his eyes. Feed him with apricocks and dewberries."

"Apricocks?" wondered Tseid, as Cobwebb asked, "Dewberries?"

Snapping with curt urgency, the captain commanded, "Just do what he asks!" She glanced toward the sensory cowl as in a softer voice she added, "While I wind thee in my arms as doth the woodbine the sweet honeysuckle so entwist; the female ivy so enrings the barky fingers of the elm."

Bottom turned and said, "Scratch my head, Mustardseed."

For a moment both bewildered crewmen stood staring mutely at their captain, normally stern and formal, now sensuously wrapping her arms around the interloper like an smitten schoolgirl. Then, as Titania slinked and purred at the man's side, Tseid fathomed her intent: the captain had taken hold of both of the man's arms with astounding subtlety.

With the Athenian held amiably helpless, Mr. Tseid stepped forward and uncoupled the wires connecting the sensory cowl's battery pack, bringing the whirling sonic dishes to a halt.

"I thank you for your courtesy, Mustardseed," Bottom said. "That tickle is well relieved."

Titania nodded approvingly. "Now, Mr. Cobwebb, fan the moonbeams from his sleeping eyes. Nod to him, and do him courtesies."

"Aye, pray you sir," Bottom said. "Fetch a lamp, for it seems the moon has gone full down, and I can barely see the nose upon my face."

With that request, Cobwebb inclined his head toward Bottom, then reached to the cowl and spun the adjustment dial, raising the darkened lenses and bringing the sensitive starlight filters into position once more.

The sudden burst of enhanced light was overwhelming. Bottom shrieked, "Heigh! Heigh! Oh, good and sweet fellows! Heigh! I beg you, undo this hateful imperfection of mine eyes!

With Bottom incapacitated, Mr. Cobwebb pulled the Aero-Sonic Sensor roughly off of his head.

"Have a care with that," Titania commanded.

Plunged from momentary blinding light to inky darkness once more, Bottom pleaded, "My lady! Where have you gone, my dear heart?"

"Think you I could be enamored of such an ass?" she asked. Still clutching one of Bottom's arms, she set her boot on his backside. "Now, churl, take your flight, and I'll tell you how you'll end this night. You will sleeping here be found by some mere'atals on the ground."

With a kick she sent Bottom reeling away from the lunathopter. His eyes were still overwhelmed by the burst of enhanced starlight within the cowl, and he couldn't see where he was going. He blundered over roots and tussocks, then finally took a tumble into the dense, tangled undergrowth of the forest where his head met the firm bark of a fallen log and he collapsed to the ground, knocked insensible.

Near the access panel, Oberon worked by the glow of a gaslamp, attaching the pneumathal to the ship's battery bank with a set of heavy conduction cables. It was a haphazard arrangement; the charging instrument had been in storage aboard the lunathopter for years. But with just a few more connections, the dreadful thing would be functional once more.

The potent essence was drained through a device known euphemistically as "the closet," a small chamber that held the victim immobile. All that remained was to find something to place within that vile chamber.

Something, or someone.

The first officer was securing the final circuit when a mechanical hum and a swirl of air heralded Robin's arrival. Though he'd seen it many times, Oberon was always amazed to watch the mantle's optical illusion at work, making the user appear out of thin air.

"Hast thou the power there, welcome wanderer?" Oberon asked anxiously.

"Aye, there it is," Robin said, guiding his hovering chair to a stop. He handed Oberon the nugget he'd found on the distant bank.

"Well done, Mr. Robin," Oberon said. "Now we may draw the needed force from this resinite and be gone by break of day."

But before he could act, Titania's voice called out, "Stay your hand, Mr. Oberon."

"Captain, let us tarry not," Oberon said. "The remedy for our spent batteries is here."

"There is more remedy necessary than this," she said as she joined them in the lamplight. Oberon felt a cold chill on his spine when he saw the Indian boy standing at Titania's side.

"What is the matter, captain?" Oberon asked.

Seeing the golden shard in Oberon's hand, Titania said, "I can see, Mr. Robin, that you made use of one of our aoratosmantles to retrieve this herbal exudant. Where, exactly, did you find it?"

"On a bank a league or more hence," he answered.

"And on this bank," the captain asked, "was there a pair of venturing Athenian youths?"

"Aye, captain," Robin said. "They did bandy over the affection of some woman, but I departed unseen at their approach."

Drawing an angry breath, Titania said, "Unseen, perhaps, but not unfelt." With that, the captain held up the Aero-Sonic Sensor she'd retrieved from the custody of the bumbling Athenian. After sending the confused man on his way, she explained, she'd recalibrated the cowl's instruments, and in so doing had picked up the sounds of the lovers' duel through the sonic relay. "You have bedazzled those two men into an infatuation with another woman. Their trivial squabble is now a passionate brawl."

"This is thy negligence!" Oberon scolded.

"They forged a deadly quarrel from their euphoric glee?" Robin wondered with a shake of his head. "Lord, what fools these mere'atals be!"

"These fools will now do each other some harm in our absence," Titania sighed. "Atlantean regulations could lay charges of murder upon us if the governance council learns one of these testy rivals has perished through our interference."

"Of that, you can be assured, Captain Titania," said

a haughty voice from the darkness.

Turning, they found the apothecary eavesdropping on their conversation from the margin of the lamplight.

Stepping closer, he continued, "I came to see if I might offer some aid in making your repairs, yet now I perceive how a small issue of mechanical failure has been compounded by your own dalliance among the simple-minded mere'atals."

"You mistake the situation," Titania said. "If you'll but return to your compartment–"

"Despite your efforts at distraction," he interrupted, "I did note your congress with that Athenian swain aboard the ship. The authorities will know of this violation when we reach port, for with each minute's delay, the crisis at home grows worse. Now, by the seniority of both Atlantean law and the oath of my profession, I demand we depart this place at once."

"Master Apothecary," the captain retorted, "Regrettable though the situation is, we must make amends ere we fly. It will take us but a small time to set both our craft and these Athenian contestants in order ere we take leave."

"Then it is fortunate for you that a swift solution is at hand," the apothecary said. "You have, as I see, a quantity of the potent resinite ambar. I know a concoction which may be brewed from it, which will relieve the hallucinatory effects that they suffer from."

Oberon asked, "How much of the ambar would be required to make your draught?"

"It takes much potency," the apothecary explained. "I perceive the nugget you have here would be just enough for two doses."

Oberon looked to Titania. They both knew what this meant: Letting the apothecary use the ambar would leave none to power the pneumathal.

The time to pursue humane alternatives was gone.

Seeing Oberon's face, Titania stifled his objection with a tiny shake of her head. "Enough trouble has been wrought by our offenses," she said. "Despite our best intents, we must mend all and be away. Apothecary, take the ambar and brew your elixir."

"Captain!" Oberon protested. "Please, if you'll just—"

"Stay your objections," Titania interrupted. "Using the pneumathal is our only course. And though none of the crew may be compelled to undergo ordeal in the name of duty, any may submit willingly."

"I do not follow," Oberon said.

"I will be the one to undergo the pneumathal," Titania announced. She glanced at the Indian boy and thought of him paging through the ship's chartbook with bright curiosity. "The potency of this boy's spirit and the life force of an Atlantean captain are equal in the effect of the device. There is wisdom in that, and I beg your patience, Mr. Oberon, that I saw it not ere now." With a dismissive pat on the boy's shoulder, she told Oberon, "I give him straight to you, that you might bear the lad to your bower and raise him in your philosophy."

The boy moved obediently to stand beside Oberon. Then, with a salute to her first officer, Titania stepped toward the pneumathal's closet. But as she did, she was stopped by a small hand on her wrist.

"Captain, why must you restore *both* of these

combative wooers?" asked the Indian boy. "If you do, they will simply pursue their quarrel over the first woman, will they not?"

"What other choice is there?" Oberon asked.

"With respect, sir," the boy explained, "If you were to restore only one of the men's sensibilities, they'd quarrel no more. Rather than discordant tension, we would depart with a perfect form of love in balance. Creating harmony could hardly be called interference, could it?"

The captain considered the boy's words. "Robin, would half the power of this resinite suffice to see us home?" she asked.

"It will, captain," Robin said with a certain smile. "I'll make it do."

"Then take the better half, apothecary," Titania ordered. "And brew your potion. Be swift. For the morning lark will shortly call, and we must be away in flight ere the lifting of the night."

"We'll fix these batteries with a charge and take the sky like russet-pated choughs at the gun's report," Robin said. With a nod, Mr. Oberon and the young mechanical now in his custody rushed off to begin their work as the apothecary retired to the confines of the ship to make his potion. "When the potion's done," Robin said, "I'll carry it to the weary lovers swifter than an arrow from a Tartar's bow. I'll leave a dram of it nearby where one of them will surely quaff it in his exhaustion. When he does, he'll find remedy, and take true delight in the sight of his former lady's eye. The man shall have his mare again, and all shall be well."

Robin saluted the captain and guided his chair up

the loading ramp to wait upon the apothecary's work.

The lunathopter's maintenance bay and loading ramp soon swirled with a flurry of activity as the first gleam of dawn grew upon the horizon. Shortly, the ship was ready for takeoff. With the batteries charged, the elixir delivered, the crew onboard, and all secured, Oberon clasped the captain's hand in congratulations as the stars faded behind the graying sky. "Thou and I are new in amity."

With a sly grin, Titania looked into the lightening woods once more. "Time for the 'ferry folk' to begone, and be all ways away."

They shared a chuckle, and together climbed the boarding ramp. Above, the impellers turned with a whine as all the crew took their places for the last leg of their voyage to Atlantis.

—⚊—

The golden light of morning lent the woods an emerald glow. As a swirling gust of heavenly air softened to a light southern breeze, the startled birds sang out their dawn chorus to greet the day.

A patch of ferny branches stirred, and suddenly a man's head appeared among the leaves.

"When my cue comes, call me and I will answer!" Bottom announced to the empty woods. "My next is, 'Most fair Pyramus!'"

His voice echoed through the forest.

"Heigh-ho!" Bottom called. "Peter Quince! Flute, the bellows-mender! Snout, the tinker! Starveling!" No voices replied; only the sighing of the wind in the treetops.

Finding a painful lump on top of his head, Bottom gave it a tender pat. "God's my life," he exclaimed quietly. "Stolen hence, and left me asleep! I have had a most rare vision. I have had a dream, past the wit of man to say what dream it was. Man is but an ass, if he go about to expound this dream. Methought I was..." he rubbed his eyes and ears, thinking he could almost still see strange lights, and feel an odd tickling sensation on his scalp.

"There is no man can tell what. Methought I was... and methought I had... but man is but a patched fool, if he will offer to say what methought I had. The eye of man hath not heard, the ear of man hath not seen, man's hand is not able to taste, his tongue to conceive, nor his heart to report, what my dream was."

In that claim, Bottom was quite correct. Bottom's friends were back at home in Athens lamenting his loss. He would find his way back and they would all be reunited before noon. Although they begged him to tell them where he'd been, when he described his time among the "fairy folk," the others would only laugh at what they believed was an imaginative jest. Bottom asked Peter Quince to write a ballad based on his adventure, but Quince refused. No sensible person, he told Bottom, would take such a lunatic tale seriously.

Years later, a young man came to Athens—a strong and healthy young man nicknamed "Broadshoulders," who had a familiarity with the lands of the Orient, and was well versed in the study of philosophy—and published a book about an advanced civilization on a distant continent. When it was read, nearly everyone believed the man's writing was a brilliant (though somewhat fantastic) parable about the roles of law and government.

Only Bottom recognized that story as anything more than allegory. Sadly, when Bottom tried to seek out the author of the book, he was turned away. Bottom was just a retired actor, and no such "ass" would be allowed through the doors of the newly established Athenian Academy, or allowed an audience with its master, the wise and learned Plato, the first to write an account of the Lost Continent of Atlantis.

"Devouring Time, wear thou steam-hammer's head"
by J.H. Ashbee

Devouring time, wear thou steam-hammer's head,
And spread craquelure on white china limbs;
Slowly strip the laboratory roof of lead,
And fade the airship's canvas by your whims.
Make gold and silver seasons as thou fleets,
And do whate'er thou wilt, high-geared time,
To London's or Constantinople's streets;
But I forbid thee one most heinous crime:
Engrave not with your hours my love's fair brow,
Nor scratch lines there with thine antique quill pen.
Him in thy course unrusted do allow
For beauty's pattern to succeeding men.
    Yet do thy worst, old time; I beat thy wrong:
    My love shall in ice-vault ever live young.

Richard, Dismantled
by Jess Hyslop

A white hart stood emblazoned in the stained glass window dominating the southern end of Westminster Hall. The creature wore a golden collar, fastened to its neck with jewelled rivets. The white hart: the sigil of King Richard II. On this day, bright sunlight streamed through the hart's breast, illuminating the beast with a celestial glow. The weather knew irony, it seemed, in the face of what was about to happen.

Henry Bullingbroke ignored the window and its symbolism. Such things did not concern him. Glass was glass, mere transparent panes to be shaped or smashed at will. He stood on the dais with his back to the window, surveying the crowd gathered in the hall. Courtiers and earls, dukes and bishops, merchants and commoners. All returning his gaze with breathless expectation. Some looked defiant, their lips hard and straight; some were nervous, their fingers entwining and their feet shifting on the cold stone slabs. But all were waiting, watching. Watching him. And he was ready to play his part.

"Fetch hither Richard, that in common view he may

surrender!" Bullingbroke's command echoed round the cavernous space. *So we shall proceed...* Bullingbroke thought, as the Duke of York—Richard's own uncle—muttered assent and hurried out. *So we shall proceed... without suspicion.*

The hart blazed, unheeded, at his back.

For a short while, silence held court in Westminster Hall. The assembly stood tense. Bullingbroke folded his arms across his chest, trying to calm the wild beating within. But there was not long to wait, for soon Richard's approach was heralded by an unmistakable clanking sound. Heads swiveled round as the clanking grew louder, and hundreds of eyes watched as the King entered the hall, adorned as ever in the Regalia.

It was difficult not to catch one's breath at the sight of him, and even Bullingbroke let out a quiet hiss as Richard paused at the top of the hall's northern steps. The Regalia was always an impressive sight, polished and gleaming, but at Richard's entrance, the sunlight fell upon his raiment and was reflected with astonishing intensity. At that moment in Westminster Hall, it was as though a figure of solar brightness stood above the assembly, a conscript of Heaven radiating light and power. Reminding them of something they'd once believed...

Heaven for his Richard hath in heavenly pay
A glorious angel. Then, if angels fight,
Weak men must fall, for heaven still guards the right.

But then Richard began his descent, and the sunlight faded from his apparel, and the illusion broke. Richard became merely a man encased in an awkward suit of armour, walking heavily down the steps. The crowd's ranks parted as he approached, forming a pathway of staring faces. As the King passed along it, his eyes were the only thing visible between his visor and his crown, but those eyes raked the assemblage with such melancholy force that many could not meet them. Gazes skittered away as cheeks heated in shame.

Finally, Richard stopped before the dais, shoulders slumped. Features schooled into a stern composure, Bullingbroke looked down upon him. Looked down upon his King.

"Alack," said Richard dully, his voice muffled by his golden visor, "why am I sent for to a king, before I have shook off the regal thoughts wherewith I reigned?" A hand twitched in a tired gesture as Richard indicated the Regalia that enveloped him.

Bullingbroke said nothing. Richard's sunken eyes flickered to either side.

"I well remember the favours of these men," he said. "Were they not mine?"

A ripple of uneasy murmurs.

"God save the King!" Richard's sudden shout echoed off the stone walls, then was lost among the dark oak rafters. He looked round, scanning the crowd. Some men looked back, but most glanced away, biting their lips.

"Will no man say 'Amen'?" Richard asked.

More shuffling of feet.

"Well then." Richard turned back to Bullingbroke, who all the while had remained stationary and impassive. Richard met his eyes. "Amen," he said. "God save the King… although I be not he. And yet, amen, if Heaven do think him me."

Bullingbroke frowned at that, and opened his mouth to speak, but Richard cut in.

"To do what service am I sent for hither?"

It was York who answered. He had quietly followed Richard down the hall, and now stepped forward to address his unfortunate nephew. "To do that office of thine own good will which tired majesty did make thee offer." He indicated Richard's Regalia, a slight tremble to his hand. "The resignation of thy state and crown to Henry Bullingbroke."

Richard's head drooped. Sweat slid down his face, hidden beneath the Regalia. He was tired. So tired. He remembered a time—could it have ever existed?—when the weight of this armour had seemed as nothing, when it had been as though his own skin. Oh, he had been a King then: impenetrable, untouchable.

The breath of worldly men cannot depose
The deputy elected by the Lord.

How bitter those words now. How hollow. Hollow as the crown that sat upon his head. Richard could feel its familiar weight pressing upon his temples, the pressure of the screws bored at intervals into his skull, keeping the precious gold in place. At coronation, as the Bishop declared the covenant between God and King, this compact was sealed for all to see as the Crownsmith took his tools and joined crown and bearer, driving gilded bolts into human head. The rest of the Regalia followed—a golden suit of arms, all riveted in place—the trappings of sovereignty. The coronation was a binding, physical contract. A contract that lifted the King from the realm of mere worldly men.

Yet it turned out that the workings of the divine

world were not so different from this one: they seized up, creaked, malfunctioned. And they could be manipulated, meddled with. Stolen.

For here was the Crownsmith once again, coming forward with his wrench in hand. Another traitor. Once the Regalia was instated on a King, the Crownsmith should never remove it for any reason save for replacing the armour as the King's size dictated. Yet now the Crownsmith was to perform the ultimate treason and heresy: to dismantle the Regalia of the rightful King.

But Richard had consented. There was no other choice. He was outnumbered, his army defected, his followers turned against him. His own *blood* had turned against him.

It seemed that blood was not enough. The Regalia was not enough. Not even a heavenly contract was enough. To be a King... What made a King? Had he been so very bad at it?

The expressions of the surrounding crowd told him: Yes.

Then I must not say no.

He was beginning to understand, now. He was starting to see that it was not God who gave him this title, this shining raiment. It was the people who had the final say. The breath of worldly men held more power than he had imagined; like dust he could be blown away.

Richard nodded. His head seemed to weigh a thousand pounds—no, more, the weight of a country— but still he nodded.

The Crownsmith advanced. Richard could feel more sweat gathering on his brow, feel his aching joints, feel the sores where over the years the Regalia had chafed his skin. His body, his weak and worldly body, was making itself known. And if the Regalia and he were not one... if it could be removed just as it was put on... on what grounds did he call himself King?

"Stop." Richard held out a hand. The Crownsmith halted. Richard turned his palm upward, his golden gauntlet gleaming. "Give it to me."

The Crownsmith glanced at Bullingbroke. The usurper stared hard at Richard for a moment, then nodded. The Crownsmith placed the wrench in Richard's hand.

A King can be undone by many things. By assassination, by incompetence, by treachery, by a foolish love. His fall can be slow and inevitable like a gnawing illness, or quick like an arrow-shot. But no matter his tragedy, his Regalia can only be undone by the tool of the Crownsmith, methodically, carefully. The disassembly of kingship takes a long time.

Westminster Hall held the crowd in hushed suspension as Richard struggled with the bolts. The crown had many fastenings, and he was forced to hold the wrench at awkward angles, unscrewing each one with ungainly lurches. Small hisses of pain echoed beneath his visor with each twist. Often the tool slipped from his clumsy grasp and clanged to the floor. The first time, York started forward to pick it up, pitying his nephew–but Bullingbroke waved him away. Bereft of allies, Richard bent to retrieve the implement, staggered in his heavy vestments, and almost fell. But he managed to right himself, and with the wrench in hand, he straightened and wearily continued his task.

Finally, the last of the bolts dropped to the flagstones, rolling away to come to rest at the foot of the dais, leaving a trail of blood behind. Richard detached the visor's joints from the crown, lifting the face-covering away and placing it on the floor. The air stroking his lips and chin felt strange and chill, his indrawn breaths dry and oddly fresh after years of breathing the trapped moisture of his own exhalations. But he did not have the luxury to dwell on this; Bullingbroke was waiting.

Raising shaking arms weak from his exertions, Richard lifted the crown from his head, gasping as he disturbed a welt decades in the making. Scabs broke and leaked fluids to join those oozing from the boltholes that punctured his skull. Blood trickled down his forehead and over his cheeks. The rim of the crown was stained. The blood of a King. But red—red like any other man's.

"Are you contented to resign the crown?" Bullingbroke's sudden question made Richard start, and he realised he had been staring in reverie at the circlet in his hands.

"Aye," said Richard, beginning to extend the crown toward Bullingbroke, who leaned down from the dais to take it. But then—"No." Richard twitched the crown back towards his body, hunching his shoulders protectively as though cradling a child. "No…" After all, this had been a part of him, a part of his very *being*, for so long. How could he part with it? Who was he without his crown, his kingship?

But the voice of reason whispered in his ear. He was defeated. There was no other choice.

Richard struggled within himself as the crowd

looked on. Bullingbroke gazed down upon him with a thunderous frown, shoulders tensed, as if ready to challenge Richard at any moment. He was too strong— far stronger than Richard, the trembling figure below. Bullingbroke was the one who conducted himself like a King, the one who had the love of the people, the one who had done right by them.

"...Aye." This time it came out as no more than a breath, but the hall was so quiet that all gathered there heard it. Richard reached up and held out the bloodstained circlet. Bullingbroke took it from him respectfully, but firmly. Staring into his usurper's steady eyes, Richard wondered if Bullingbroke was really as sure of his right to kingship as he seemed to be. What lurked beneath that stony countenance?

Well, they were about to see what was behind Richard's own trappings. And not even he could remember what that was.

"I resign to thee," Richard told Bullingbroke, then once more reached for the wrench. "Now mark me how I will undo myself..."

For that was how it felt as Richard took the wrench to the Regalia's bolts and removed its heavy pieces one by one, grimacing as the screws wound out of his flesh. A chant swirled around his mind as he did so, keeping him from focusing too much on the pain:

I give this heavy weight from off my head,
And this unwieldy sceptre from my hand,
The pride of kingly sway from out my heart...

Shining armour clattered to the floor. Vambraces, rerebraces, greaves, poleyns, cuisses, spurs, faulds, backplate, breastplate...

*With mine own hands I give away my crown,
With mine own tongue deny my sacred state...*

All eyes watched as Richard stripped himself of the Regalia, stripping himself of the identity he had taken for granted for so long.

With mine own breath release all duteous oaths...

Finally, Richard stood quivering in the vaulted hall of Westminster, shivering in the stained and stiffened rags that had gradually rotted away beneath his royal attire. A small, bleeding, stinking, defeated man.

But for all that, a small smile touched his lips. "'God save King Henry,' unkinged Richard says, 'and send him many years of sunshine days!'"

Confusion clouded Bullingbroke's features; was this sad creature mocking him?

Richard cocked his head, making his lank, matted hair fall straggling over his bloody forehead. "What more remains?"

Clearing his throat to mask his distaste at the stench rising from Richard's unwashed body, the Duke of Northumberland stepped forward from the crowd with a parchment in hand. "No more," he said, "but that you read these accusations and these grievous crimes committed by your person and your followers against the state and profit of this land. That, by confessing them, the souls of men may deem that you are worthily deposed."

Northumberland's voice grew more certain as he spoke, his faith in the rightness of his words helping him to overcome the shock of seeing the true face of his erstwhile King. Such a wasted, pale face...

And it had grown paler as Northumberland's words

echoed round the hall, answered by mutterings and even shouts of agreement. The mention of Richard's crimes had enlivened the spectators, making them stand straighter, remembering why they were there, remembering why they had supported Bullingbroke in his rebellion. Richard himself had seemed to wither as Northumberland spoke, the hint of a smile vanishing as quickly as it had come.

"Must I do so?" Richard addressed not Northumberland but Bullingbroke, standing with crown in hands. "Must I ravel out my weaved-up follies?"

Bullingbroke stared back, implacable.

Northumberland took this as permission to approach Richard. "My lord, dispatch! Read o'er the articles." He thrust the parchment toward the former King, who took it with an automatic gesture.

Unrolling the paper and gazing down at the long list scribbled upon it, Richard's shoulders grew still more hunched, his chin drawing towards his chest.

"Mine eyes are full of tears, I cannot see," he mumbled, then drew a shaking breath. "And yet salt water blinds them not so much but they can see a sort of traitors here." At that, he raised his head and glared at Northumberland, who gaped in surprise at the sudden ire that had kindled in Richard's eyes. "Nay!" Richard cried, clutching the parchment in both hands and throwing the words out in fits, "if I turn mine eyes upon myself, I find myself a traitor with the rest!" Confusion filled the hall, the gathered people unsure whether Richard's anger was aimed at them or at himself. "I have given—*here*" —Richard flung aside the parchment and spread his arms wide— "my soul's consent to undeck the pompous body of a... of a *King!*" This last he spat with such derision that it unnerved almost all who heard it. That word—king—what did it mean any more?

Recovering from his shock, Northumberland scrambled for the parchment. "My lord—"

"No lord of thine, thou haughty insulting man!" Richard cried. "No, nor no man's lord. I have no name, no title— no, not that name was given me at the font— but 'tis usurped!"

Anger and anxiety rippled through the crowd. Yells of "Quiet him!" contested with dismayed murmurs. Bullingbroke raised his hands, trying to restore calm. He seemed to be readying himself to speak, but Richard was not yet done.

"If my word be sterling yet in England," Richard shouted over the din, "Let it command a mirror to me straight, that it may show me what face I have, since it is bankrupt of his majesty!"

Seeing that Richard was not to be hushed until he'd had his say, Bullingbroke gestured brusquely to his aids. "Go some of you and fetch a looking-glass," he growled. An attendant hurried out.

Northumberland stepped forward again, doggedly proffering the parchment. "Read o'er this paper while the glass doth come," he urged Richard.

Richard swiped the document away. "Fiend! Thou torments me ere I come to hell!"

Northumberland looked helplessly at Bullingbroke, who gave a curt nod. "Urge it no more, my lord Northumberland."

"But—the commons will not then be satisfied!"

Northumberland protested.

"They shall be satisfied," Richard said. "I'll read enough when I do see the very book indeed where all my sins are writ—and that's *myself.*"

Eyeing the unpredictable Richard, Northumberland finally backed down, just as Bullingbroke's attendant returned bearing a handheld mirror.

"Give me that glass," ordered Richard, "and therein I will read."

The attendant bowed as he handed over the mirror, and then seemed to realise what he was doing. He cast a guilty glance at Bullingbroke before scuttling out of sight.

Taking the mirror in hand, Richard raised it to his face and confronted his new, exposed self. Staring back at him were a pair of dark, deep-set eyes, surrounded by a band of tanned skin where the light had been able to penetrate between the crown and the visor of the Regalia. The rest of the face was a clammy, unhealthy white, tracked with oozing blood. His lips were thin and chapped, his teeth yellowing; sores clustered at the corners of his mouth. Like a corpse's visage. Like a man who had been clad in gold so long he had forgotten he was already dead.

How could this man have been divinely chosen? He was nothing more than wasting flesh hanging on the bone. He was nothing.

And yet, Richard had expected worse. Ever since that day at Barkloughly Castle (*let us sit upon the ground...* he had cried in his despair), that day when he realised that his army had abandoned him, that he was defeated, he had become slowly and painfully aware of the creaking, wounded body hidden within the Regalia's bright casing (...*and tell sad stories*...). More and more he had felt the grinding of the bolts within his muscle, scraping against his bones, his skull. No matter how often his servants tended to his never-healing wounds, no matter how hastily they wiped the Regalia clean, he witnessed the gradual leaking of his blood (...*of the death of kings*...).

"No deeper wrinkles yet?" he whispered, a melancholy breath that misted on the mirror and reached no further. "Was this face the face that every day under his household roof did keep ten thousand men?"

What fools they all were, Richard realised with a sudden shock. What fools they *all* were–he, Bullingbroke, his countrymen–to bow to a suit of armour, even a golden suit of armour, when what lay beneath might be... might be someone like *him.* Richard managed to tear his gaze away from his own ravaged face, and looked up into Bullingbroke's. Strong, hard–what some might call noble. A fitting face for a King, the people must think, to allow this man to break the sacred tradition of divine right that had held sway so long in England. But they were wrong. There *was* no fitting face for a King. The title meant nothing, the lands meant nothing, even the Regalia meant nothing– the *appearance* meant nothing. Why dress oneself up in gold, as if that changed anything about oneself? Kings could only prove themselves in deed. At that, Richard had failed. He squinted hard at Bullingbroke, who gazed back with that inscrutable expression. Did he have it in him? Who could tell? Richard, unable for so long to even read himself, certainly could not.

Richard did not look back at the mirror, but let it fall to the floor where it crashed into a hundred pieces, scattering and shattering, the shards throwing out multi-hued light in a dizzying array—just for a moment—then all was still.

"As brittle as the glory is the face," Richard said hoarsely. "Mark, silent King, the moral of this sport—how soon my sorrow hath destroyed my face."

This was the only small redemption Richard could perform as one-who-had-been-King, the only form of apology he could give Bullingbroke, the man he'd wronged and exiled. The warning was obscure, but it was there, if only Bullingbroke could comprehend it. If he *wanted* to comprehend it.

Upon the dais, Bullingbroke's gaze had followed the mirror's descent, blinking as it broke upon the flagstones. Then his cold, grey stare rose again, raking Richard's ailing countenance.

Was that a spark of understanding in Bullingbroke's eyes? A twitch of nervousness from his lips? A wrinkling of the brow that presaged the heavy wrinkles still to come?

Richard hoped it was enough.

"I'll beg one boon," said Richard, "and then be gone and trouble you no more."

"Name it, fair cousin." Bullingbroke's voice was soft, thoughtful. A good sign, Richard thought.

"Give me leave to go."

"Whither?"

"Whither you will, so I were from your sights."

Westminster Hall was a breathless cavern of

tension. Even the white hart in the window seemed to be poised, intent on the scene below. This was Bullingbroke's moment, and the people waited to see what he would do. How to treat an unkinged King? What kind of judgement could a traitor lay upon the man whom he betrayed?

Bullingbroke remained still, but the damp sheen that covered his forehead revealed the struggle churning within. Richard's previous words weighed heavy in the air, like a mist clinging to the earth.

Then: "Convey him to the Tower," Bullingbroke said, his words like iron, like locks and keys and prison bars. Like despair.

Richard cried out as the guards surged forward and laid their hands upon his feeble body. Their merciless grips seized on once-sacred flesh and they dragged him roughly out, his bare heels scraping along the flagstones. The crowd milled and muttered, swallowed and nodded, hid their faces and cried. There was wetness on York's cheeks as his nephew's cries faded away. The echoes died soon after, absorbed into the stones of the hall. It was a chamber that had seen many things, both magnificent and terrible, and would see many still to come.

In the midst of the confusion, Bullingbroke stepped down from the dais. The crown flashed in his hand, catching the light from the window; its boltholes seemed to wink.

Bullingbroke gestured to the Crownsmith, who stood patiently by. The man approached, retrieving his wrench from where Richard had abandoned it. "Are you certain that this is your wish, my Lord?" he asked Bullingbroke, speaking with a heavy gravity. "Once done, it–" He paused. "It is *difficult* to undo."

Bullingbroke thought of the fluids that spattered the floor, and the shards of glass that crunched beneath his feet. He remembered Richard's expression as he had looked into that mirror. Some revelation discovered there.

As brittle as the glory is the face.

The dismantled Regalia lay bloody on the ground. The discarded pieces formed a haphazard jumble that seemed to suggest some pattern, some symbol that Bullingbroke might read–*should* read–if only he knew how. The stray bolt still rested at the foot of the dais. An invitation, or else a warning.

About the Authors and Sonneteers

Jennifer Castello is a fiction writer, playwright, and editor. Originally from Nebraska, she moved to Chicago to obtain her degree in playwriting from The Theatre School at DePaul University. Her scripts have been performed nation-wide, including the American Theatre Company (Chicago) and LA Circus Theatricals (Los Angeles). Her first novel, The Messiah of Howard Street, was published in 2009. For more information, please visit www.jennifercastello.com.

Olivia Waite was making up stories for years before it occurred to her to write some of them down. She's had three short historical romances out in the past year, with more on the way. When not writing, she is often found singing karaoke with her brilliant husband, or making jewelry with a mini-dachshund curled up beside her on the couch.

A young writer hailing from deep in the ancient forest of Sherwood, on the borders of England's industrial North, ***J.H. Ashbee*** has dabbled in poetry prose and many things besides. He prefers however writing for Mr. Edison's new-fangled cinematron, principally in the genres comic, historic and actionic. Preferring to keep his affairs to himself, little else is known about him; even whether he's using his real name.

Rebecca Fraimow lives in a box in Brooklyn with two roommates and a tragic lack of cats. She has in the past been paid to do such things as copyediting, seamstressing, fundraising, and conference organizing, and is currently a neophyte film preservationist, blogger and fiction author. Her work has previously appeared in Steam-Powered II: More Lesbian Steampunk Stories.

Tim Kane lives and teaches in Chula Vista, California, with his spectacular wife, daughter, and a double fanged dog. He grew up on H. G. Wells and the giant creatures from Toho. He still fears that the Beast Folk will steal him in the night. His stories come from the splinters that lodge in his brain. His first published book, The Changing Vampire of Film and Television, analyzes the past seventy years of vampires. Other stories have appeared in Legendary Horrors (Anthology), Verbatim, Far Sector SFHH, and Fish (Anthology). Check out more at www.timkanebooks.com.

Tucker Cummings is the author of "The Strange Adventures of Margery Jones," a microfiction serial about parallel universes. Her work has been featured online at HiLoBrow.com (where she took first prize in their Spooky-Kooky fiction competition), Fiction365, and OneFortyFiction. Her other credits include "Future Lovecraft" (Innsmouth Free Press), "Stories in the Ether" (Nevermet Press), "Grim Fairy Tales" (Static

Movement), "Daily Flash 2012" (Pill Hill Press) and "The Thackery T. Lambshead Cabinet of Curiosities" (Harper Collins). Visit her online at tuckercummings.com, or say hi to @tuckercummings on Twitter.

Bret Jones is an Associate Professor and Program Director of Theatre at Wichita State University in Wichita, Kansas. His duties include teaching acting, directing, and scriptwriting. He has been writing for a number of years and has had novels published and plays produced. He is also a writer, actor, and producer for The Ancient Radio Players, an audio theatre group based out of Oklahoma.

Frances Hern divides her time between Calgary, Alberta and Golden, British Columbia. She loves Calgary's sunny skies and Golden's incredible scenery and outdoor activities. She writes poetry, fiction and non-fiction. Her poems have been published in anthologies that include Red Berry Review, Silver Boomers, Freefall, Freckles to Wrinkles, Poems for Big Kids, This Path, Home and Away and Crave It. Her published non-fiction titles about Canadian History are Norman Bethune, Arctic Explorers, and Yip Sang and the First Chinese Canadians. Check out www.franceshern.ca

Ruth Esther Jane Booth (Miss) is a clerical assistant, freelance critic of the Arts, and penny bag hawker from the North-East of England. Her work has previously appeared in such esteemed publications as Kerrang! Magazine and The Independent; the electronic journals

Thrash Hits, Virtual Festivals and The Escapist; and a great many more worthy newsheets.

In her spare time, Miss Booth enjoys chaperoned travel, prestidigitational obfuscation, and is a keen student of the varied uses of radium-infused cornstarch.

Alia Gee's eyes are nothing like the sun; they're more like a grassy meadow being sucked into a starless vortex of hopeful angst. She spent one whole afternoon in Stratford-Upon-Avon and somehow managed to completely miss visiting their world famous Teletubby Museum and Shop. She now lives in New York City growing heirloom tomatoes, writing about revolutions, and teaching her kids to say please.

Claudia Alexander studies the planets and flies spacecraft by day. By night she re-imagines the universe. She has written a number of steampunk short stories, children's science-learning books, and a full length elf-punk novel. She is also an avid tennis fan and has written for the Bleacher Report as claudiacelestialgirl. Red Phoenix Books, her publishing arm, was established in 2002.

When *Larry Kay* cleans the foul Tampa-by-the-Bay soot from his goggles, he is thankful his beautiful wife has not left him for a cleaner man that does not smell of engine oil and phlogiston. If you liked his SteamShake entry, look for more lip-smackin' wordsmithy at ScribbleNinja.com. Remember: "Keep calm and unfurl the escape ropes off the dirigible."

Kelly Ramsdell Fineman was born in the suburbs of Chicago, Illinois. She earned a B.A. from Susquehanna University and has a law degree from Georgetown University. She lives in Cherry Hill, New Jersey, and has won awards from Writer's Digest for her work. Her poems have appeared in Mountain Magic: Spellbinding Tales of Appalachia, in journals, and in books for the commercial and educational markets. Her first picture book, At the Boardwalk, was published by Tiger Tales Books in March, 2012.

Scott Farrell is a performer with San Diego's Intrepid Shakespeare Company's "Shakespeare for a New Generation" Educational School Tour. His forthcoming novel is "The Champion In Silence," an adaptation of a 13th century legend about the only woman to ever sit at King Arthur's Round Table. When not writing or acting, Scott is the director of an educational outreach program called Chivalry Today (www.ChivalryToday.com) and his presentations on themes of knighthood and chivalry have been given to the San Diego Shakespeare Society, Sisters In Crime Mystery Writers, Romance Writers of America, and as part of the California Public Library's Summer Reading Programs.

Jess Hyslop is a young British writer with a particular passion for fantasy and science fiction. In 2010, she won Cambridge University's Quiller-Couch prize for creative writing with her short story 'Augury', which is now available through Shortfire Press. Her fiction has also appeared in Bewildering Stories, Cast of Wonders, and Abandoned Towers. She is currently at work on a novel.

About the Editors

Jaymee Goh is an aca-fan and writer of speculative fiction, blogging extensively on the use of steampunk to explore postcolonialism. She has contributed to Tor.com, The Apex Book Company Blog, and BeyondVictoriana.com. Her words have been quoted in *Steampunk II: Steampunk Reloaded* and *The Steampunk Bible*. She has fiction in Crossed Genres, Expanded Horizons, and Steam-Powered 2, and non-fiction in *the WisCon Chronicles 5 & 6*.

Matthew Delman developed an appreciation for Shakespeare during his teen years, when he first read Julius Caesar in English class. He is currently the Publisher of Doctor Fantastique Books and the Publisher/Executive Editor of Doctor Fantastique's Show of Wonders magazine, where their goal is to be "Reporting on the Steampunk world, one cog at a time."